LIGHTS OUT

Fargo hit the ground as bullets whirred above his head. He spotted two of the outlaws and snapped off accurate shots, driving them back. Like a snake, he worked his way in the direction McGhee had taken, but he worried he was too late and the outlaw leader too fleet of foot. Then the other two deputies suddenly appeared from behind, shooting in the air, driving the gang out of the brush.

Hope surged in Fargo's breast. They could take the outlaws right here and now.

Fargo poked his head up, lifted his rifle, and got Mustang Jack in his sights as the two deputies flushed him out like a wild turkey. He heard the report and wondered at the sound when he had not pulled the trigger yet. Then he felt the sudden sharp pain in his skull.

The Trailsman slumped forward, unconscious.

SIGNET
Published by New American Library, a division of
Penguin Putnam Inc., 375 Hudson Street,
New York, New York 10014, U.S.A.
Penguin Books Ltd, 27 Wrights Lane,
London W8 5TZ, England
Penguin Books Australia Ltd, Ringwood,
Victoria, Australia
Penguin Books Canada Ltd, 10 Alcorn Avenue,
Toronto, Ontario, Canada M4V 3B2
Penguin Books (N.Z.) Ltd, 182–190 Wairau Road,
Auckland 10, New Zealand

Penguin Books Ltd, Registered Offices:
Harmondsworth, Middlesex, England

First published by Signet, an imprint of New American Library,
a division of Penguin Putnam Inc.

First Printing, August 2001
10 9 8 7 6 5 4 3 2 1

The first chapter of this book previously appeared in *Dakota Damnation,*
the two hundred thirty-seventh volume in this series.

 REGISTERED TRADEMARK—MARCA REGISTRADA

Printed in the United States of America

PUBLISHER'S NOTE
This is a work of fiction. Names, characters, places, and incidents either are
the product of the author's imagination or are used fictitiously, and any
resemblance to actual persons, living or dead, events, or locales is entirely
coincidental.

THE

TRAILSMAN

#238

CHEROKEE JUSTICE

by

Jon Sharpe

A SIGNET BOOK

1

Skye Fargo rode slowly on his Ovaro, entering Fort Smith, Arkansas, from the north. The road was dusty and the day muggy. Clouds building in the south promised rain to take the edge off the stifling summer heat, but Fargo knew better than to count on a downpour. This time of year Arkansas was well known for its changeable, erratic weather.

But the weather was nowhere near as unpredictable as his old buddy Coot Marlowe. Fargo had been trading hard-won buffalo hides for not enough money up in St. Louis when he had received the telegram urging him to come visit for a spell. Coot had a knack for finding men, and had unerringly located him almost a year after they'd parted ways up in the Dakotas. Fargo had been sorry to see Coot go, especially to become a bounty hunter. While tracking down owlhoots might be a job that needed doing, Fargo thought Coot could better use his skills out in the Rockies or up in the Bitterroots.

Still, Arkansas was a green, lush place and seemed hospitable enough. And wherever Coot was, there were always plenty of wide-eyed does willing to curl up with him in his bedroll.

Fargo wiped the sweat from his face with his faded blue bandanna and then held a hand up to shade his eyes. As he rode, he noted the deserted streets, empty houses and vacant stores. It was as if Fort Smith had been driven off by some unknown threat. Fargo wondered if that might be possible until he heard the distant buzz of a large crowd toward the center of town. He turned his Ovaro and saw more and more people hurrying in the same direction, like ants invading a spill of sugar on a kitchen table.

"What's the big ruckus?" Fargo called to a bespectacled man locking his bookstore before joining the trail of men and women.

"You jist ride in, mistuh?"

"I did, sir," Fargo said.

"They's gonna hang that son of a bitch. Nobody wants to miss that!" Without further explanation, the man hurried off, his short legs pumping hard to keep himself moving at the same speed as the others around him.

Fargo had seen his fill of executions, but the chance that Coot was there too, kept Fargo moving in the direction of the Fort Smith town square. The large open area held a gazebo and next to it a large gallows loomed like a wooden vulture waiting for someone to die. Men milled around the gallows doing this and that, but most focused their attention on the half-dozen well-dressed men in the gazebo.

Fargo heaved a sigh. He recognized the politicians immediately. They took every chance they could get to make a speech, no matter that desperados were going to get their necks stretched for crimes so horrible women fainted and strong men blanched.

"There you are," came a familiar voice. "Figured you'd be here in time to see the fireworks."

"They shoot off firecrackers at executions in Fort Smith?" Fargo asked. He dismounted and went to his old friend. Coot Marlowe about crushed him with a bear hug, and Fargo returned it. They slapped each other on the back and then pushed apart.

"You're a sight for sore eyes, Fargo. You ain't changed a bit, 'cept you don't smell like a buffalo anymore. What happened? You run into a rain shower on the road?" Coot was a huge man with an even bigger appetite. Fargo had missed him sorely.

"No rain," Fargo said, knowing he was being joshed. "I hitched my wagon to a couple of those big catfish out in the Mississippi and let them pull me along so I'd arrive all fresh and rested."

The trail dust and the lather on the Ovaro's sides put this to the lie, but the two had always swapped tall tales. Fargo remembered fondly when Coot had once told him how he'd had a mule that died during an especially hot summer in Nebraska. The corn in the field had popped from the heat, leaving a white blanket close to two feet deep as far as the eye could see. The mule saw this, and not being too bright, thought it was snow and froze to death on the spot. It had taken Fargo a week to come up with a topper.

"Come on around here so we can get a good look at the festivities," Coot said, guiding Fargo through the fringe of the crowd and down a side street. They weaved in and out of narrow alleys and back streets until emerging again not fifty feet from the gallows.

"You have something to do with the man who's going to hang?" Fargo asked.

"Funny that you should say that," Coot said, grinning crookedly. "As a matter of pure fact, I was the one who tracked 'im down and brought 'im back to Judge Ringo."

"Judge Ringo's the presiding judge in these parts?"

"A fair man but over his head when it gets down to enforcin' the laws. He has political aspirations reachin' far from these fine rollin' hills, with an outlaw lurkin' behind every one."

"Heard tell the lawless element is running wild here," Fargo said. "Why's that when a man like you is here to chase them down?"

"Injun country, that's why," Coot said, turning sober. "They head into Indian Territory knowing that the United States Army can't go after them."

Fargo sucked in his breath. He had the feeling Coot's telegram had meant more than wanting to get together for another bender and to reminisce about old times.

"I'm not a bounty hunter," Fargo said. "Let the law go after criminals. I'm content to—"

"There," Coot said, grabbing his friend's arm with an iron grip. "See that one with the smirk on his face. He still don't believe he's gonna die."

"What'd he do?"

"That's Jason Strain, 'bout the most vicious killer I ever saw. First he killed a man, then his two sons and then raped a woman 'fore killing her too. And that was only for practice. When he was plyin' his trade, he was even meaner."

For a moment Fargo thought Coot might be exaggerating, but the solemn note in his voice spoke the truth as he saw it, with no embellishment.

Even worse, he's got himself a gang to run with. They do their dirty work over here in Arkansas and then hightail it into Indian Territory where there's not much law."

"What about the cavalry at Fort Gibson?"

Coot snorted in disdain.

"They couldn't find their own asses if they used both hands and had a first class scout helpin' them. Oh, they send out patrols and fight sorties, but mostly they try to keep the Five Civilized Tribes safe from the wild Indians on the western frontiers."

"The Osage?"

"They kick up a fuss," Coot agreed. "So do the Arapahos and the Comanches. The cavalry boys don't have much time to track down killers and thieves from outside Indian Territory."

"You want me to partner with you to get the rest of Strain's gang?"

"Hell, Fargo, he ain't even the leader. I can't even call him the worst. I know what you think about bein' a bounty hunter, but look at it more as doin' a public service."

"One that pays well?" Fargo couldn't keep a small smile from creeping to his lips. Coot always had an eye out for the ladies—and a quick buck.

"This one I'd do for nothin'," Coot Marlowe said, and Fargo believed him. Coot looked Fargo square in the eye and said, "I found those dead settlers and saw what Strain'd done. After I brought him in, the rest of the gang went wild and burned out close to twenty other settlers."

Fargo saw that Coot blamed himself for the arson spree.

"That wasn't your fault," Fargo pointed out.

"Not catchin' them was. They're good, Fargo, better'n me." Fargo stared silently at his friend. Coot had always

4

considered himself the best there was at whatever he did. Knowing that this bear of a man admitted to being second to a gang of killers was enough to send a shiver down Fargo's spine.

"They're not better'n the Trailsman," Coot finished. "Money doesn't mean that much to you, Fargo. I know that. But I swear on my mama's grave, every dime of reward money we might get is yours. I'll do this for nuthin' but the pleasure of seein' them varmints strung up."

Fargo nodded, then said, "You never had a mama. You crawled out from under a wet rock."

The crack was enough to break Coot's somber mood, as he let out a laugh. "I knew I could count on you, Fargo. Now why don't we watch the law take care of that vermin."

Fargo saw that the politicians had stopped their speech making but refused to give up the moment. They moved to the edge of the crowd, shaking hands and howdying with the men standing up close. Fargo's eyes drifted from the crowd to the gallows—and lower.

He frowned, trying to understand what wasn't right. Men milled around like bees swarming on a brightly colored flower.

"You know them?" he asked Coot.

"The deputies? Most of 'em. Judge Ringo doesn't do too good a job hirin' the best, but then the pay's pretty bad."

"They're practically tripping over each other." Fargo said. "That's a lot of law for just one hanging."

"I told you Strain was a mean son of a bitch." Coot answered, his voice raised so Fargo could hear him over everyone else.

The level of excitement among the Fort Smith masses rose to a pitch until the air was charged, like before a summer storm. "That's Judge Ringo," Coot said. He pointed out a smallish man with a big handlebar mustache and a towering black stovepipe hat preparing himself to address the crowd. The judge wore a plain broadcloth coat and maintained the appearance of a hellfire-and-brimstone preacher ready to unload a sermon.

In spite of his diminutive size, the judge's voice

boomed like thunder as it broke over the crowd. A hush fell as everyone succumbed to the man's spell. Coot had said Judge Ringo had political aspirations and Fargo could believe it. The man had a way of holding the crowd's attention, even if he was only relating what they all knew.

"I have seen some mighty heinous crimes in my day," Judge Ringo began, "but those committed by Jason Strain are by far the most reprehensible. I take no pleasure in witnessing his execution, because it does not bring back the men and women that he has wronged so grievously. To ask for God's mercy on such a malignant soul would be an outrage upon the almighty. His voice cracked and roared like thunder as he turned to the condemned man and shot him a scornful look. "Jason Strain," the judge bellowed, clearly playing to the keyed up mob. "As the swing of the trap door begins your downward path to hell, all I have left to say to you is good riddance!"

A cheer went up as a curiously calm Jason Strain mounted the gallows steps. He went to the center of the gallows and stood on the trapdoor as easily as if he went waltzing out in a barn dance.

"Something's wrong," Fargo said. He felt it in his gut even though he was uncertain how to respond to it.

"Nothing can go wrong, they bought new rope just for this execution," Coot told him. "Hell, I would have loaned them my own if they'd needed it."

The execution proceeded. The executioner pulled a black hood over an unresisting Jason Strain's head and moved the condemned into position. A noose was placed over Strain's head and just as the executioner was about to tighten it everything went to hell.

"There!" shouted Fargo, pushing forward. A spark caught his eye as one of the deputies struck a lucifer and applied it to a short length of black miner's fuse. Immediately he went for his Colt as the fuse sputtered and sizzled its way toward a large mound draped in cloth.

Fargo shouted a warning and Coot joined in, but they were too late, as kegs of black powder hidden under the gallows exploded. Both men were thrown back, stumbling as they crashed to the ground. Fargo tried to keep the gallows in view throughout the chaos since he knew what was coming next.

The pounding hooves of a half-dozen horses completed the story. The outlaws in Strain's gang had come to rescue him. Blowing up the gallows had been a distraction so they could carry him off. It was the perfect plan, or it would have been if not for one problem. The explosion had reduced the gallows to splinters—and in the process it had blown Jason Strain to kingdom come! The man lay like a broken doll over the beam that had been intended to hold his noose. The executioner moaned and thrashed about as the cross beam pinned his legs to the ground. Two deputies at the base of the gallows had died outright in the explosion, along with the outlaw who had lit the fuse.

"The danged fools used too much explosive," Coot said, struggling to his feet. "Get 'em, Fargo. We can still get the rest of the gang!"

Five riders scattered the crowd, shooting into the air and at any lawman they came across. They reached the blown-up gallows and wheeled about until they were sure Strain was dead. Two of the masked outlaws argued, apparently over whether to leave their partner or to take his body.

Good sense prevailed and the five galloped off, leaving behind the sixth horse that had been intended for Strain.

Fargo let out a whistle as Coot Marlowe sprinted for the horse, grabbed the saddle horn and pulled himself up. The horse bolted and Coot fought to get a good seat. Fargo wasn't waiting to see how his partner was doing because if any man could stay on the spooked horse, it was Coot. As the Ovaro approached, Fargo swung onto it and lit out past the sundered gallows at a dead gallop, hot on the heels of the retreating outlaws.

"That way," shouted Coot. "They went that a'way!" His considerable weight slowed down the horse intended for the much lighter Jason Strain, letting Fargo rocket ahead.

Head down to cut the air knifing past him, Fargo followed the cloud of dust kicked up by the fleeing outlaws through the streets of Fort Smith and out to the edge of town. His Ovaro was flagging from such heavy service, but Fargo knew there wasn't a horse on either side of the Mississippi with more heart. He closed the gap between himself and the road agents gradually—when he caught wind of an ambush.

Three outlaws rode ahead, slowing down considerably. Their horses had to be tired, as was his, but Fargo knew the two missing road agents had not had a chance to break off down some cross street.

He ducked as a bullet whistled through the air where his head had been only an instant before. Riding low, using the Ovaro as a shield, Fargo got out his Colt and returned fire. The horse dug in its heels and came to a dusty stop in the middle of the street, giving Fargo a better chance at hitting something now—and giving the outlaws a better chance of hitting him.

He had already fired three times. He had two more rounds left, preferring to leave the hammer resting on an empty chamber while traveling in hot weather. Fargo had to make the shots count. And he did.

His last round spun around one of his attackers. The owlhoot grabbed his gun arm and turned the air blue with profanity.

"Get him, get the bastard!" the wounded man shouted to the others in his gang.

Fargo swallowed hard when he saw the three who had been bait for the trap ride back, their six-shooters out and ready to ventilate him. He shoved his six-gun into its holster and grabbed for his Henry. The rifle hammer tangled in a dangling leather strap as he pulled it out. More frantic now, Fargo tugged harder and jerked the rifle free.

With the trio almost on top of him he knew he could take out at least one and possibly two, leaving the last outlaw standing to sign his death warrant. Fargo knew he was a goner, but he was determined to take as many of them with him as he could.

The round in the chamber misfired, giving off a dull *pop!*

He levered in a new round as the thunder of hooves came over him, only the hoofbeats in question came from behind. Coot Marlowe had finally caught up with him. The bounty hunter shouted and made as much noise as he could to distract the ambushers from Fargo.

Coot succeeded in drawing their attention. He opened up with his six-gun and threw the outlaws into confusion.

"We got 'em on the run, Fargo. We got 'em where we want 'em!" Coot cried enthusiastically. Those were his last words.

The three riders fought their bucking horses. Fargo had already wounded one of the ambushers on foot, but the other stepped forward, leveled his black powder Remington, and fired. Fargo watched in slow motion as the puff of white smoke belched from the muzzle. Coot threw up his hands, twisted, fell from the saddle, and landed hard a few yards from where Fargo stood helplessly.

The moment dripped by like a bead of molasses on a jar. Fargo lifted his Henry and fired. His aim was off, but it was enough to send the man who had gunned down Coot Marlowe scuttling away like the rat that he was. Fargo fired wildly at the other three, but continued to miss. In the smoke of stray shotgun blasts, they decided retreat was better than facing the enraged gunslinger.

Fargo turned back to the pair of outlaws. He had already winged one. He could at least even the score by downing the one who had shot his partner.

They were nowhere to be seen.

Fargo stepped up, his rifle ready for action, and there was not a target to be found anywhere.

Then he heard the cold voice from behind.

"Drop that rifle or I'll drill you. I swear I will!"

Fargo had no choice. He lowered his Henry and waited for the slug in the back that would end his life.

2

"If you so much as twitch, I'll cut you down where you stand," came the cold command. Fargo felt like doing more than twitching. He felt like chasing down the men who had killed Coot Marlowe.

"I—what you want me to do, Mr. Thomas?" came a shaky voice.

"Hog-tie him and we'll take him back to the marshal."

"Marshal?" Fargo looked over his shoulder. The two men with their six-shooters trained on him both wore tin stars on their vests. One had a hard look to him and the other was hardly out of his teens. The young man's eyes were wide with fear, and he held his six-gun as if it might bite him.

"Who'd you think would be arresting you for killing Coot Marlowe?"

"He was my partner. I'd never do anything to hurt him." Fargo looked at Coot's body and felt cold inside. outlaws who gunned him down won't get away with it. died saving me. I swear, they won't get away with killing him!"

"Mr. Thomas, you reckon he *was* Mr. Marlowe's partner?"

"Of course he wasn't. He's lying to save his worthless hide. He was one of them hurrahing the townspeople and trying to save Strain."

"My name's—"

Deputy Thomas cut Fargo off with a curt movement of his six-shooter.

"Get moving. You got an appointment with the marshal, then the judge, and finally the gallows. It looks like we're gonna get to see a hangin' after all!"

Fargo scooped up his Ovaro's reins and walked slowly, hands up, while the two deputies trailed him. Every step of the way to the marshal's office was a source of pain for him. Coot had died saving his life, and right now there was nothing he could do to avenge his partner's death.

"Inside." Thomas said.

"Should I come with you?" asked the wet-behind-the-ears deputy.

"Get on out of here," Thomas said. "I can handle this from here."

Fargo started to tell the deputy he was wrong again, then swallowed the words. The marshal was the man to convince, not a man as easily mislead as Deputy Thomas.

"What you got for me this time?" asked a scrawny man behind a large desk. As he turned, a silver badge beaten out of a Mexican silver peso flashed.

"He killed Coot Marlowe. Reckon he's one of the gang, Marshal," Thomas said.

"You were a Texas Ranger?" asked Fargo, eyes on the badge. He could not read the inscription from across the room but the design was familiar.

"I was. You find trouble down in Texas, too?" demanded the lawman. "We might have ourselves a real reward if we can rustle up enough wanted posters on this one."

"I scouted for Company B in the Texas Panhandle. Captain Greer."

"So you know a name or two? I'd expect that from a gent one step ahead of the law."

"My name's Skye Fargo."

"I don't care if your name's—" began the deputy behind him, still holding the six-shooter aimed at his spine.

"Hold on," the marshal said, standing. The man was so skinny he'd look like a needle if he closed one eye. He fixed a steely stare on Fargo. "You lie about that and I'll kill you myself."

"Who's Fargo?" asked Thomas.

"Shut up," snapped the marshal. His eyes bored into Fargo's lake-blue ones. "Who are you again?"

"Skye Fargo. Some folks call me the Trailsman, and Coot Marlowe was my partner. I got a telegram from him asking me to come to Fort Smith. I'd just met up with him when the outlaws tried to save Jason Strain."

"How'd you know the varmint's name if—"

"Shut up, Thomas," said the marshal. He waited for Fargo to explain.

"Coot said he brought in Strain. He told me all about his crimes and how hard it was tracking the rest of the gang down because they always hightailed it for Indian Territory. I'd agreed to help him find their hideout."

"Can you prove you're the Trailsman?"

"In my saddlebags is the telegram from Coot. It's got my name on it."

"Go check his gear," the marshal said to Thomas.

"This isn't right, Marshal Packer. He—"

"Git your carcass moving. Now!" Packer rested his bony hand on the butt of a worn Smith & Wesson, saying nothing more, keeping his unyielding gaze fixed on Fargo. Less than five minutes later Thomas returned with the telegram.

"It's like he said. This is addressed to a man named Fargo, but how do you know it's him?"

"Tell me about Greer," the marshal said, his hand still on the butt of his gun. Fargo saw that his reply meant the difference between getting locked up for killing Coot or going after the real murderers.

"Greer always carved a notch every time he caught a criminal," Fargo said.

"Nobody notches the handle of his six-shooter," scoffed Thomas.

"It wasn't his gun," Fargo said. "It was a piece of willow about eight inches long. He confided in me he would retire when he had filled up the entire length. When I left him in Texas, he only had an inch or so to go."

"I don't reckon Greer ever told anyone he didn't trust with his life about that stick," Packer said, taking his hand off his six-shooter. He motioned impatiently to his deputy to put away his hogleg. "The man's telling the truth."

"If you say so, Marshal," Thomas said with ill grace.

"I do," snapped Packer. "Set yourself down, Fargo. Tell me what happened after the explosion."

Fargo spent the next ten minutes relating what he and Coot had seen and done. He finished by saying, "Coot wanted us to track them down for the reward. Keep the reward, Marshal. I'll find them and bring them back for nothing."

"It won't be for nothing," Packer said. "It'll be for the good of all Arkansas. They are about the most vicious killers I ever come across, and I've seen some wild ones."

Fargo noticed that Deputy Thomas had left. That suited him just fine.

"Marshal, anything you can tell me about these out-laws will be appreciated."

"It's hard to know where to start. Their leader's a snake named Mustang Jack McGhee. He's a tough case, but his right-hand man is just as bad, if not worse. That'd be Ned Sondergard."

"I've heard of Sondergard," said Fargo, thinking hard. "He held up a bank in St. Louis a few months ago. The law's looking for him there."

"The law's looking for him in a lot of places. He and McGhee teamed up in Indian Territory while they were hiding out, and the territory's never been the same. They draw killers like horse shit draws flies." Marshal Packer looked up as the door opened.

Thomas held the door open for a short man with a big mustache.

"Judge Ringo," Fargo said, rising and sticking out his hand. "Coot Marlowe pointed you out to me."

"I heard what the McGhee Gang did to him. A great man, Coot Marlowe," the judge said in a baritone belying his stature. He looked past Fargo to the marshal. "I see you and Marshal Packer are off to a good start. Have you identified Coot's killer yet?"

"I got a good look at him, but I can't put a name to the face," Fargo said.

"Here, look at this," said the judge, taking out a yellowed, brittle wanted poster from a coat pocket.

Fargo's hand involuntarily went toward his holster. He caught himself in time and relaxed a mite.

"That's the man."

"That there's Mustang Jack McGhee," said Packer, looking over Fargo's shoulder.

"I want him behind bars," Fargo said, resolve hardening. "Then I want to see him swing for killing Coot."

"Bring him in, Mr. Fargo," said the marshal, "and me and the judge'll do the rest."

Fargo fumed as he waited for the two deputies to gather their gear and prepare for the trail. Marshal Packer had insisted on sending along Thomas and another deputy named Delacroix so any arrest in Indian Territory would be legitimate.

"Do not fret so much, Fargo," Delacroix said in his heavy French accent. "It is not so easy becoming a federal deputy in these parts."

"I'm glad Judge Ringo is such a stickler for details," Fargo said sourly. He didn't see why either the judge or the marshal couldn't deputize him so he could go on his own without having the two deputies dogging his footsteps.

"The appointment of any deputy, even this simple thing, takes months to come from Washington. It is what you call very political and a prized position," Delacroix said, cinching the belly strap on his saddle tight enough to make his horse try to buck. The deputy held the horse down and soothed it.

"This might be why there's so much lawlessness out here," Fargo said. "Was Coot a deputy?"

"Your Coot, he was quite a man, eh?" Delacroix worked on twirling the sharp tips of his mustache. Fargo thought if the Cajun deputy used any more grease on his pencil-thin mustache it would slide right off his face.

"But he wasn't a deputy?"

"No, he was not," Delacroix said. "He operated, how do you say, with a letter of marque?"

Fargo had no idea what Delacroix meant. The Cajun brightened as he figured out another way of explaining to Fargo. "He was a bounty hunter with extra-legal authority. He broke the law but did good so the marshal and Judge Ringo looked the other way."

Fargo wondered why he couldn't operate the same way. Then he knew. Coot was quite a talker and had probably sweet-talked his way into being trusted. Knowing Coot he probably slept with the governor's wife and got her to put in a good word for him with her husband. No matter how much admiration Marshal Packer had for Fargo's reputation, the Trailsman was a possible source of trouble and the marshal would see him that way until he came to know him personally.

For his part, Fargo did not intend to stay around Fort Smith that long. He wanted Coot's killers brought to justice and then he could move on.

"You ready to ride?" Deputy Thomas looked at Fargo as if he had bitten into a bitter persimmon.

"Where do McGhee and his gang usually hole up?" asked Fargo, climbing into the saddle. He settled his weight and the pinto stallion began prancing, as ready for the hunt as Fargo.

"They've got a couple of hideouts across the river, in Indian Territory. Unfortunately they've got more places to hide than we've got deputies to look for them," Thomas said with no enthusiasm.

"But no!" cried Delacroix. "They would not be there. Not yet. They thought they would be six, no? Surely they would have planned to rob and kill a bit more on this side of the Mississippi. Then they return to lick their wounds on the other side of the big, muddy river."

"What wounds?" asked Fargo. "If they steal a pile of gold, doesn't that make them winners."

"Ah, but Jason Strain is dead," Delacroix said with some satisfaction. "It is not every day that McGhee suffers a loss."

"What kind of loss is it when you lose a man who'd

15

as soon shoot you in the back as look at you?" asked Thomas.

Fargo saw the two deputies would argue endlessly about where to go without ever moving from the stables. He got his horse out into the bright Arkansas afternoon and looked around. The town square was a likely starting place if he had to track McGhee's gang from the gallows—but he decided where he had been ambushed was better. The number of feet and hooves obscuring the trail would not be as distracting.

Besides, the fleeing outlaws had set the ambush for him without hesitation, telling him they knew that part of town pretty well. He headed for it, cutting down back streets and making his way toward the spot where Thomas had stopped him earlier. The two deputies followed his cue.

"What do you expect to find here?" Thomas asked. "There's no way in hell you could track those varmints from here."

The deputy sounded petulant. Fargo ignored him as he went to the ground and began hunting for any trace of McGhee and his outlaw band. He paced from one side of the street to the other and verified what he had guessed. There had been no indecision on the part of the two men who had separated from the gang.

"They've ambushed folks here before," Fargo said, looking up at the two mounted lawmen. They had remained astride their horses, letting him do the work in the dirt.

"You can tell that? Why, you are a phenomenon!" cried Delacroix. "I must tell my grandchildren of this day!"

"You don't even have any kids," grumbled Thomas. "What makes you think there'll ever be any grandkids if you keep scaring women away like you do with that ugly face of yours?"

Fargo let the two argue. It was not the good-natured banter he and Coot had enjoyed, but different men developed different bonds. He had the feeling Thomas and

Delacroix had ridden together before and that this was their way of getting along.

He dropped to his knees and studied the ground again. The tracks in the street had been erased by traffic after the ambush. Even the bloody patch in the dust where Coot had died was gone, trampled by boot and hoof. But on either side of the street he found traces of where the outlaws had waited to catch him in a cross fire as he raced after the other three.

No hesitation finding the spots, no milling about to discuss the matter. That told Fargo this road led toward a hideout, probably temporary, that the gang protected. Mustang Jack McGhee was a man who planned ahead. That made him even more dangerous.

Then Fargo laughed out loud.

"What is so funny?" asked Delacroix.

"McGhee is quite a planner, yet he let his men put too much black powder under Strain's gallows."

"Yeah, right, that's rich," muttered Thomas.

"You know McGhee?" asked Delacroix.

"I'm going to know him a damned sight better before I bring him in," Fargo said, his blue eyes fixed on the road out of Fort Smith. It led due west. McGhee had a back way out of his hidden camp that led straight across the river into the chaos swirling around the Five Civilized Tribes.

"Why do you ride this way?" asked Delacroix, urging his horse to greater speed to keep up with Fargo. "You have their trail?"

"That's not possible," said Thomas. "Look at the road. We need rain. This dust don't take tracks too good. Hell, it don't take tracks at all! We're on a wild-goose chase. I tell you, they'll head north first, before crossing."

"I think we go in the wrong direction," Delacroix said, agreeing obliquely with his partner.

Fargo let them bicker like a pair of old women. He kept on the road going west from town. McGhee had come this way with the idea of escaping. Two of his men had been prepared to lay down covering fire as they escaped with Strain. That part of the plan had gone awry. But the rest of the retreat went well.

It had gone so well that it had left Coot Marlowe dead.

The buildings became farther apart and soon Fargo rode in the lush Arkansas countryside. The hills rose around him, blocking any view farther than a mile or two. A man could get lost in these rolling hills real fast. An army could vanish in this land and no one would be the wiser. It was about perfect for McGhee's gang.

Fargo kept this in mind as he scanned the ground for tracks. He hunted alongside the road for any trace that the outlaws had left the dusty thoroughfare and taken to the hills, and listened hard for any unnatural sounds. If McGhee had left a sentry behind, the birds might take note and not sing.

All Fargo heard was the heavy drone of insects buzzing about his head. He swatted idly at them and kept riding. He found an area of cut-up grass where more horses had been tethered, giving the escaping gang that much better a chance against pursuit. The road still led west.

Across the river and into Indian Territory.

For two days Fargo rode with the pair of deputies fussing the whole way.

Fargo heaved a deep breath as he stared at the wide, sluggishly flowing river.

"I see why they call it the Big Muddy," he said. "How do we cross?"

"The same way McGhee would have, if he had come this way," griped Thomas. "We find a barge to get us across."

"We should not cross," Delacroix said. "The gang did not come here. They are somewhere else in Arkansas, killing and robbing. We are on the wild-goose trip."

Fargo had nothing solid to present as an argument. His gut instinct told him McGhee and his men had come this way. Unfortunately, after finding the corral where the outlaws must have penned their spare, fresh horses, he had seen nothing to tell him this was the proper trail to follow.

"Let's find a barge and get across." Fargo's tone brooked no debate. The two lawmen rode silently, giving him a respite from their sniping at each other. For a while.

"There is a ferryman nearby," said Delacroix, "but he is a thief. He will ask too much. If we go a few more miles upriver we can find another."

Fargo ignored Delacroix's advice and trotted to the sleepy-eyed man with his feet hiked to the top of an overturned bucket as he leaned back against a shed that might have been his home.

"Afternoon," Fargo greeted. "We need to cross."

"Thass good," the man said, getting his feet down, "because I need the money." He pushed his hat back and peered at Fargo. "Yep, figgered you'd be by."

"How's that?" asked Fargo.

"Them others. The ones in such a hurry to get across. They had the look of being on the run from the law."

"And I look like the law?" Fargo didn't know if he should be amused or ecstatic at being right about the men who had already crossed the Mississippi. He was positive the ferryman meant Mustang Jack McGhee.

"Those fellas do." The ferryman pointed at Delacroix and Thomas.

"This the man who crossed earlier?" asked Fargo, holding out McGhee's wanted poster so the man could see it. The man nodded curtly.

"How much for the three of us and our horses to cross?" asked Fargo, waiting for Delacroix's prediction to come true.

"You federal deputies? Well, I'll get you across for nothin' if you promise to arrest them fellas. They robbed me. As if I'd ever ferry them across again!"

Fargo looked at a disgusted Delacroix and Thomas, then urged his Ovaro forward onto the gently rocking flat-bottomed barge to begin the trip across the Mississippi into Indian Territory.

"When do we rest?" complained Thomas. "We been on a false trail for damned near a day since crossing the river and I feel like my ass is turning into one giant blister."

Fargo looked over his shoulder and saw no real discomfort on the deputy's face. If he was as inexperienced a horseman as he claimed, he would be in real pain by now.

"We're getting close," Fargo said. The expression of surprise on Thomas's face took him aback.

"How do you know this thing?" asked Delacroix, his voice level and controlled. The Cajun deputy's hand went to the six-shooter holstered at his hip, as if he was prepared to shoot it out with McGhee's men then and there.

"I don't think McGhee would have his hideout too far from the river. Far enough, but not too far," he said with some conviction.

"You cannot be serious," Delacroix scoffed. "They would not stay here! Why, they would run like the wind once across the Mississippi to safety! To the far side of Indian Territory. By now they must be in Colorado!"

"They're around here somewhere," Fargo said. He felt it in his bones. He reined back and looked to his left. Fargo took a long, deep sniff of the air and caught the faint hint of coffee boiling. A half mile off rose a twisting, turning column of smoke about right for a campfire. Up on a ridge stood a tree that had been struck by lightning, but the smoke definitely came from a cooking fire. While the camp could be any traveler through this part of Arkansas, he would bet money that he had found where McGhee and his gang had gone to ground.

Not waiting for the two arguing deputies, he switched his reins across his Ovaro's shoulders and got the horse trotting in the direction of the campfire.

"Wait, Fargo!" cried Delacroix. "Where do you go?"

"To catch the bad guys," the Trailsman said with a smile. And if it was not McGhee and his men, Fargo wanted to find a Cherokee to learn what he could of the territory. For a full day they had ridden hard from the river and had not seen anyone. It was time to change that.

"Wait!" came Thomas's order. "We need to stick together."

Fargo was past catering to the pair of deputies and their constant bickering. He wound his way through a stand of sweet gum trees, slowing as he neared the camp. Fargo's heart jumped into his throat when he spotted a man outside the camp pissing against a tree.

"McGhee!" he cried, going for his six-gun.

The man jumped, turned and saw Fargo coming for him, Colt leveled. He tucked himself in and dived for cover in time to avoid the slug that ripped a chunk out of the tree he had been using. Fargo was usually a better shot, but had gotten buck fever at seeing his friend's killer so unexpectedly.

Fargo rode hard, rounded the tree and ran the outlaw leader down quickly. The man fumbled to get his six-shooter out, but he had to hitch up his gun belt and try not to slip on the debris-strewn forest floor as he ran.

Coming up to him, Fargo kicked out and sent Mustang Jack McGhee stumbling to the ground. Fargo wheeled his pinto and pointed his pistol squarely at the fallen man.

"Lose your smoke wagon," he said, sighting down the barrel of his Colt. "Lose it or forfeit your miserable life."

"Who the hell are you?" demanded McGhee from the ground. He considered his situation, then clumsily tossed aside his six-shooter.

"I'm the man taking you back to Fort Smith to stand trial for killing Coot Marlowe."

"Marlowe? Who's that?" McGhee started to button up his fly.

The movement distracted Fargo from the real danger. He had been so intent on going after McGhee that he had forgotten the rest of the gang. From the corner of his eye he caught movement in the thick undergrowth. Fargo swung around and fired, winging one outlaw. Three others opened fire on him.

"Get him, boys. He's the law!"

Fargo tried to plug McGhee before he could get away, but the deadly fusillade from the outlaws forced him to duck low as he rode for cover in a stand of trees. He got off a couple of shots in McGhee's direction, but the outlaw scampered away about the time Fargo's Colt came up empty.

Thrusting his six-shooter back into his holster, Fargo unlimbered his Henry. The rifle barked once, twice, three times. The outlaws lost some of their taste for fighting. Or so he thought.

As Fargo tried to locate McGhee again, the road agents opened up with rifles and shotguns. He realized he had bitten off far more than he could chew and jumped to the ground, then dodged behind the sticky sap-oozing sweet gum trees, hunting for sanctuary.

He fell belly down on the ground and took a quick peek around the tree to locate his attackers. Fargo spotted two and got off accurate shots that drove the outlaws back. Like a snake, he worked his way in the direction McGhee had taken, but worried he was too late and the outlaw leader too fleet of foot.

From behind he heard galloping horses. He chanced a quick look and saw Delacroix and Thomas waving their six-shooters in the air and whooping and hollering like a band of Indians.

Hope surged in Fargo's breast. The three of them could take the outlaws.

Fargo poked his head up, lifted his rifle and got Mustang Jack McGhee in his sights as the deputies flushed him like a wild turkey. He heard the report, wondered at the sound when he had not pulled the trigger yet, and then felt the sudden sharp pain in his head. The Trailsman slumped forward, unconscious.

3

Fargo floated in a world of pain and vertigo. Try as he might he could not sit up. Sharp daggers stabbed into his head and turned him nauseous. He pushed his hands down against the ground and felt nothing. It was as if he had drifted away from the earth.

A distant thought came to him that he must have been killed and now made his way to heaven. Or, with so much pain, maybe he was going in the other direction. Knowing there was only one way to tell, Fargo fought to open his eyes.

More pain stabbed into his head. Light filtered through a green canopy and blinded him. Blinking furiously to clear his vision, he saw the answer to his question.

"Heaven," he said, smiling. "You must be an angel."

"Do not try to speak," came a distant voice as soft and soothing as wind in the tall pines. "Rest. Soon you will be well. I promise."

Fargo's tongue felt ten times too large. Water dribbled across his lips and into his cottony mouth before he slid over the brink into blackness again. But he knew everything would be all right. The dark, beautiful angel had promised him.

Fargo came awake with a start. Nothing was as it should be. He sat up and caught the edge of the bed as the room spun in wide, wild circles. As it settled down, he noticed a blanket had fallen off his chest. He was bare to the waist—and lower.

He looked up as a petite woman came in carrying a bowl of soup. She saw he was awake and beamed.

"You are back in the land of the living," she said, setting the fragrant soup on a table beside the bed.

"I know you," Fargo said. "You're the angel who came to me when I died." He frowned in confusion. He tried to remember everything that had happened and found it was all a blank, except seeing this young woman in his dreams.

"I am quite real," she said. "My name is Anna Three-killer, and this is my father's home."

"You're Cherokee?"

She smiled and Fargo got dizzy again. This time he wasn't sure it was completely from his wound. At the thought, he reached up and touched his head. New pain lanced through him, forcing him to lie back down.

"You need to heal. Do not rush it," Anna said.

"What happened? I was chasing outlaws and shot at them and . . . and I don't remember anything after that."

"My brother Seth found you as he came back from Tahlequah and brought you here." Anna sat on a low stool beside the bed, hands folded in her lap. Her soulful dark eyes never left him—or his nakedness. He went to pull up the blanket but her slender-fingered hand shot out and stopped him.

"It is a warm day. You do not want to become overheated."

"Just looking at you makes me mighty hot," Fargo said. "I'm sorry," he apologized immediately. "That's no way to talk to a lady who saved my life."

"We thought you had been shot by Stand Watie's men. They are everywhere between here and Tahlequah, causing mischief and harassing anyone who supports John Ross."

Fargo heard the undercurrents of Cherokee politics. He did not recognize the names, but figured Anna and her family had no love for Stand Watie, whoever he was. He had heard of John Ross, the Cherokee's elected principal chief.

"White men shot me," he said firmly. "Outlaws from Fort Smith killed my partner. Two federal deputies and I came across for them and—"

24

"Do not tire yourself with explanations now," Anna said. "My father and brother are gone now. Tell them all this later when you're stronger." The woman's hand moved across his bare chest, igniting feelings in him Fargo knew he could do nothing about now. His head throbbed and his vision doubled.

"You are too kind," Fargo said. He felt Anna's hand moving lower, under the blanket, and then he passed out again.

"You are welcome to stay until you can ride again," said Benjamin Threekiller. "My daughter says you are mending fast."

"I'm a mite shaky but getting better daily," Fargo said. "I can do some chores around your spread to help pay back your kindness."

"Heal," Benjamin said. "My daughter knows of such things. She says you had a concussion and such a wound heals slowly."

Fargo looked from the man to his son, Seth. The younger Threekiller glared at Fargo as if he were a devil with horns.

"I need to move on as soon as I can to catch the outlaws." Fargo frowned, wondering what had happened to the two deputies. "If the lawmen with me didn't already capture them."

"There wasn't anyone with you," Seth said. "I found you out on our land, spilling your blood onto our soil."

"Seth," Benjamin said sharply. "He's not a Stand Watie supporter."

"Watie traffics with the whites over in Fort Smith. He would have us align with the Southerners."

Fargo waved this off. "I don't care about Cherokee politics. Truth is, I'm not exactly sure where I am. I trailed the killers across the Mississippi without regard to where they headed."

"You are ten miles east of Tahlequah, the Cherokee capital," Anna said quickly, cutting off her brother's angry words. "John Ross lives not far from here." She smiled and added, "His home is so pretty."

"Ross lives at Rose cottage," Benjamin said. "We go there often for parties."

"This is a nice house," Fargo said. The home was well-furnished, built of sawn planks and had a decent pitched roof, unlike so many sodbusters' homes up north in Iowa and Kansas. How anyone could live in a sod hut, burrowing like a mole into the ground was beyond him. In contrast, the Cherokees—or at least the Threekillers—lived in a home that would be the envy of anyone he had met in St. Louis.

"There are small chores for you to do," Anna said, dark eyes fixed on him. "If you want."

"I do. I cannot repay you for saving my life, but doing what I can will go a ways toward thanking you." Fargo was at a loss to figure what had happened. He had caught McGhee and his gang, they had shot it out after he had gotten overly eager to capture the killer, then he had been hit in the head. He thought he remembered hearing Delacroix and Thomas riding up, but he couldn't be sure.

The lawmen might have captured the McGhee gang, but that didn't seem too likely. They would not have left him for dead. More likely, McGhee and his henchmen had killed the deputies and left them for dead. But Seth had not mentioned finding their bodies. Too much of the gunfight was a mystery waiting to be solved. When he could ride without falling out of the saddle due to dizziness Fargo knew he must return to the gang's campsite to see what, if anything, had been left behind.

"You look distraught," Anna said.

"The trail will be cold," Fargo said. He looked out the glass-pane window and saw a gentle rain falling, as it had done most of the day. A day or two of wind would erase most tracks. The shower completed what the other elements had started.

"Father," Seth said impatiently. "We must go into Tahlequah. John Ross needs our advice."

"Both Father and Seth are on the tribal council," Anna said proudly.

"Yes, you are right," Benjamin Threekiller said, looking at his pocket watch. He moved like an old man, although he didn't seem to be much past his mid-forties.

After he and her brother left, Anna heaved a deep sigh and sat with her hands folded in her lap.

"Father takes on too much."

"Considering his health?" Fargo asked.

"Is it so obvious he is sick? Yes, I suppose so. I have trained as a nurse in Pennsylvania schools, but there is so little I can do for him. Cherokee doctors can do nothing. Neither can white doctors from Fort Gibson."

Fargo started to say something more but the words proved more elusive than a will-o'-the-wisp. Anna stared at him with her dark eyes, her thoughts unreadable. Not for the first time, he saw how lovely she was. The words he wanted to say boiled up inside, only to be driven back when a new wave of light-headedness hit him, forcing him to lie down. Anna tucked him in and then he drifted into a fitful sleep.

Fargo wiped at the sweat on his forehead, then stepped back to study his handiwork. He and Seth had worked all morning to put up the fence that had been knocked down by a cow intent on escaping to dine on greener grass.

"You do good work," Seth said grudgingly. He had hardly spoken since they had come out to repair the fence, but the young man seemed to be relaxing a mite.

"Thanks. You've got a powerful lot of work to do. I'm surprised you don't have any hired hands to help out."

"Watie uses slaves. We don't believe in that."

"That doesn't mean you can't hire some help," Fargo said, perching on a fencepost like a crow.

"Help is scarce. Too many men ride in the militia, shooting at each other."

"Hadn't heard anything about that," Fargo said. "It sounds like you ought to settle your differences and unite against the Osage and the other Indians on your west border. That'd keep the cavalry out of your territory."

"You see much," Seth allowed. "But we can never

agree with Stand Watie. John Ross is our leader, and we will follow him!"

"That's all well and good unless it splits the Cherokees apart, and that's what is happening." Fargo hopped down, feeling the need to relieve himself. He headed for a stand of post oak when he heard riders approaching. Fargo finished his business and stepped out, only to freeze in his tracks.

Four riders circled Seth. One poked him with the muzzle of his rifle. Another kicked at the young man, sending him to his knees. Seth tried to dodge, only to be hit in the head by the man wielding the rifle.

Fargo slid his Colt from its holster and walked back to where the four Cherokees circled the fallen man like they were hurrahing a wagon train.

"Can I help you?" Fargo asked loudly. The four riders jumped, their attention completely on their prey.

"They're Watie's men," Seth grated out.

"Die, white eyes," cried the leader. Before he could lift his rifle and point it at Fargo, he found himself staring down the barrel of a cocked, aimed Colt.

"I don't want to kill you, but if you give me a good reason I'm sure I can be convinced," Fargo said.

"Kill him!" cried the leader.

"You'll die first," Fargo pointed out. "And one or two of your friends are likely to get ventilated, too." The steadiness of his voice and the unwavering aim he took on the Cherokee settled the matter.

The riders wheeled about and galloped off without another word.

"Are you all right?" asked Fargo, helping Seth to his feet. The young man had a deep cut on his head but was otherwise unharmed.

"You see how they are? They probably tore down our fence to let our cattle out."

"Let's get you to the house," Fargo said. The entire way back Seth grumbled about Stand Watie and his brutal followers.

"Seth, what happened?" cried Anna, rushing from the whitewashed house.

"He had a run-in with some of Watie's men," Fargo said. "But he ran them off just fine." The little lie brought Seth around, his dark eyes fixed on Fargo.

"That's not true," Seth said. "He saved me from them." Seth straightened and thrust out his hand. Fargo shook it, but the young man pulled back quickly, as if he had done something wrong.

"Get him cleaned up," Fargo said. "He might be ready for a nap after that."

Anna laughed at this and looked at him, her eyes dancing. "Perhaps you need some time in bed, too."

Fargo was not sure how to answer—or if he should in front of her brother. Anna helped Seth while Fargo hauled water from the well for the evening meal. He sank to the rear porch step when she came out and sat beside him. Her warm thigh pressed into his.

"Thank you, Skye. You saved my brother from serious injury or perhaps even death. They're terrible men, those criminals riding with Watie."

"Seth was doing a good job of defending himself," he said.

"He talks. Seth is many good things, but he is not a man of action." She half turned and looked at him. "You are a man of action, aren't you?"

Anna's dark eyes closed as she tilted her head back. She wanted him to kiss her—and more. Fargo felt the stirring in his loins and knew one kiss would never be enough.

"I'm not so much on talking," Fargo said, moving closer. "Is this what you want?"

A small smile danced on Anna's lips, then she whispered, "From the first instant I saw you!"

He kissed her. Their lips crushed together as the passion that had built between them came rushing forth. Fargo felt the woman's breasts press into his broad chest and knew he had reached the point of no return.

He moved from her lips back along the line of her jaw, kissing and nibbling as he went. He caught her earlobe and gently nipped at it, then worked to the back of her slender neck. She trembled in his arms.

"Yes, Skye," she whispered huskily. She reached out and slid her hand under his shirt, lightly moving over his chest. Then she sneaked lower, slipped out and pressed intimately into the mound growing at his crotch.

"What about your brother?" he asked as he traced around her ear with his tongue.

"He's asleep. But we can go to the barn." She began kneading the growing pillar of flesh now trapped almost painfully in his pants.

"Lead the way," he said.

She flashed him a lewd grin, turned and hiked her skirts, showing him that she wasn't wearing anything beneath. Then she dropped her skirts and ran to the barn.

Fargo reached the barn at the same instant Anna did. Laughing, breathless, they melted into each other's arms.

"I'm glad I was following you. That was a mighty fine sight," he told her. Fargo bent lower and began drawing up the woman's skirts. His fingers touched bare flesh as he worked, cupping both hands around her firm buttocks. Fargo pulled her in hard to his body and kissed her again. Their mouths locked and tongues danced while he fondled her delightful posterior.

Anna lifted a leg and hooked it around his waist, pulling her crotch even tighter against his body. She shifted a little to catch his upper thigh between her legs. Anna began rocking, stimulating herself on his leg, leaving behind dampness wherever she crushed down.

Fargo used the fleshy mounds of her cheeks to lift her entirely off her feet and swing her around. Losing his balance when she hiked her other leg around his waist, he tumbled on top of the woman into the fragrant straw in the first stall. She wiggled back, spread her legs in wanton invitation and held out her arms to Fargo.

"Hurry, get out of that gun belt—and your pants," she giggled.

Fargo took his time. His manhood throbbed with need as it stood erect between his legs, but he felt like a kid in a candy store. Everything about Anna aroused him, and he wanted to sample every morsel fully.

He grabbed a slender ankle and jerked, flopping Anna

flat on her back. The woman laughed when he began kissing up her leg, moving to her soft inner thigh. The laughter turned to soft moans of delight as he licked even higher toward the dark, furred triangle nestled between her legs.

Fargo thrust with his tongue, sampled the salty tang of an aroused woman, then moved away, working his way down her other leg. He kissed and licked and stroked until Anna's entire body trembled.

"So nice, Skye, but I want more. I want *you*!"

She ripped open her blouse, showing her naked breasts. Fargo wanted to pounce on them like a cougar on fresh kill, but he held back. He finished his erotic exploration of her legs before moving up. The delay caused the beautiful Cherokee woman to desire him even more.

He fought down the urges in his own loins as he kissed her heaving belly before working upward on her luscious body. His fingers caught at the hard nipples capping her breasts. He squeezed and rolled the rubbery buds around until he robbed Anna of all coherent speech. She panted and moaned and reached out, her hands stroking through his hair, across his face, through his beard. Then she got her hands behind his head and pulled his face down.

He dived down, kissing her breasts. At the crest of her left mound of succulent flesh he used his tongue to push the throbbing nip down as hard as he could. He felt her frenzied heartbeat through the flesh. Then he sucked hard and drew the tender point into his mouth where he teased it using his teeth and lashing tongue.

"Now, Skye, I can't stand any more. Now, please, ohhh!"

Her legs lifted invitingly on either side of his powerful body. Fargo positioned himself between her raised legs as he reached the limits of his control. She was a gorgeous woman and seeing how excited she had become, how much she wanted him, pushed him to the point where only one thing would satisfy them both.

Her legs rubbed restlessly along the sides of his body as he moved forward. The engorged tip of his shaft pressed hotly into the woman's nether lips. For a moment, Fargo paused, making sure he was ready. Then his hips shot forward. He sank all the way into the woman's molten interior.

Anna gasped and lifted her buttocks off the straw as she ground herself into his crotch. She took him deep within her most intimate recess. He felt as if he had thrust into a heated glove, with a strong hand all around him. Then she began using those hidden muscles to squeeze and release, to stimulate and milk him.

Fargo withdrew slowly, relishing every inch as he retreated. When only the head of his manhood remained within her tender lips, he shoved forward again. The friction of his passage warmed him and set his body on fire. From the way Anna thrashed and moaned beneath him, Fargo knew he was igniting the same feelings in her.

Faster and faster he stroked, the carnal heat mounting to the point where he could not stop even if he wanted.

"Yes, oh, yes, ohhh!" Anna cried out. She clawed at his back as she lifted her hips up in an attempt to take even more of his steely shaft into her body. They strove, at first with different rhythms, then growing together to reach their climaxes.

Fargo's release came as the woman cried out in an ultimate unleashing of her desires. They kept up the frantic movement until Fargo began to melt and Anna's passions abated. Sweating and tired, they sank to the straw, arms around each other.

"Thank you," Anna said.

"You've got that backward," Fargo told her. "You're enough to put a man back into his sick bed."

"Oh, really? I didn't think any part of you was weak. Now this looks tired out, though. Maybe I can revive it." She dived down to his groin and enmouthed his limp organ.

They spent the rest of the afternoon in the barn until the only energy they had left was for sleep.

4

"I can make the trip, Father. I am fine!" protested Seth Threekiller. He sat up in bed, moved his feet to the floor and tried to stand, only to turn as white as a sheet and wobble. Fargo knew how he felt. It had taken him almost a week to recover from a similar head wound.

"You listen to your sister," Ben said, glancing in Anna's direction. Her eyes were on Fargo rather than her brother. "She's got the medical training and nursed our new friend back to health. She will do the same for you."

"But the council meeting!" Seth cried. "I can speak out against Watie and his pirates! My vote is necessary or he will take over the tribe."

"I can argue on your behalf," Benjamin Threekiller said solemnly. The older man looked half past dead, but he kept running on sheer determination. Fargo wondered what ailed him. Anna had not known, nor had any of the doctors, either Indian or white.

"I'll escort him into Tahlequah," Fargo said. "I need to see if there's any word about the two deputies who rode with me." He did not add that he wanted to pick up the latest gossip about McGhee and his gang. The instant he heard of their location, he would be off like a shot. He had quite a score to settle with them. Killing Coot Marlowe was bad, but leaving him for dead only added to Fargo's need to capture them and get them into Judge Ringo's court in Fort Smith.

"I . . ." began Anna. She swallowed and then asked, "May I go, too, Father?"

"No, stay with your brother. And keep the shotgun

handy. I don't want Watie's men burning us out while I'm gone."

Fargo hesitated then. He had to find Mustang Jack McGhee and his gang, but had not considered how dangerous it was leaving Anna alone with her injured brother.

"Do you think Watie will try to burn you out?" Fargo asked.

"He has tried with others near us," said Ben Threekiller, shrugging it off. "I am sure he will come here sooner or later. When he does, I want to be ready for him."

"The quicker we get opposition organized, the safer we'll all be," Seth said.

"Then let's get your pa into town so your principal chief can do something about Watie," declared Fargo. As he left, Anna crowded close behind him and even reached around to press the palm of her hand against his crotch.

"Hurry back," she whispered, giving him one last fond squeeze before going to a gun case and taking out a double-barreled shotgun. She expertly broke it open and thrust two shells into the chambers before snapping it shut.

"I'll be back as soon as I can," Fargo promised.

He hurried outside to mount his Ovaro. Ben Threekiller was already on the road to the Cherokee capital and it took Fargo a few minutes to catch up to him.

Fargo was not sure what to expect of the Cherokees' main city, but this was not it. St. Louis didn't have such well-kept buildings or show so much wealth. The Cherokees were prosperous enough to have their own bank and, from what Fargo could tell, every imaginable business including two large churches at the outskirts of town. The one thing that took him aback were the signs.

"What are those funny curlicues?" he asked Benjamin Threekiller, pointing to signs all along the main street of town.

"We have our own alphabet," the man said. He smiled

and pointed to a building whose glass window was covered with the strangely bent lettering. "We even have our own newspaper. Sequoya invented the alphabet before the Trail of Tears, when we were still one tribe back in Georgia." The sadness in the man's voice told Fargo that he remembered when the Cherokee were settled up and down the eastern seacoast.

"That's the town hall, isn't it?" asked Fargo. The three-story white building dominated the square and most activity centered on its broad double doors.

"Yes," Ben said. "It is our courthouse and town hall and any other name for a meeting place, as we require. John Ross and the governors are here today, so it is also our council headquarters."

"You wish Seth had come along, don't you?" asked Fargo. "He's quite a young man."

"He will be chief one day. He has good sense, unlike most of the men. Moreover, he has heart and worries about our people. When he learns how to help them, also, he will make a great chief."

Fargo did not have to hear the rest of Benjamin's muttered praise. His son cared for the Cherokees—and men like Stand Watie did not. Whatever the cause of the rift in the Cherokee nation, it went deep and would be difficult to heal.

Ben dismounted, handed the reins to Fargo and strode like a conqueror up the front steps and into the town hall. Fargo fastened Benjamin's horse and his pinto to a nearby tree and followed. Again, Fargo found himself surprised by the display of wealth. Not even Judge Ringo's courthouse had such finely polished wood and well-appointed offices.

Fargo had to admit he was also taken aback because he had expected a council tent with half-naked men sitting around a fire chanting. The Cherokees dressed better than most men in St. Louis and, if Anna was any indication, many were better educated.

"He will bring us to ruin if he continues to attack his neighbors," insisted Benjamin Threekiller. The man to whom he spoke looked to be ninety years old. Frail, the skin on his hands like dried yellow parchment, John Ross nodded solemnly. But for all the infirmity of age, there was a sharpness in his eye and a certain turn to his head that showed that the Cherokee's principal chief missed nothing.

"I have spoken to him," Ross said to assuage Ben. "Then I sent John Drew to persuade him to disarm and send his militiamen back to their farms."

"He won't listen!" cried Benjamin Threekiller.

"He refuses to manumit his slaves, too," John Ross said tiredly. "My slaves have been freemen for more than a year."

"What can I do? What can you do for me? My son, Seth, was attacked by Watie's rowdies."

John Ross sucked in his breath and said, "I had not heard. Is Seth well?"

"He is healing. They would have killed him if it hadn't been for Skye Fargo." Ben turned to face Fargo, who stood to one side of the door of the council chamber. Fargo nodded politely.

"We must deal with Watie," Ross said. "Go back to your farm, my dear friend. Rest assured the full might of the Cherokee nation will fall on Stand Watie if he harms one hair on your head, or that of any of your family."

Benjamin Threekiller was not mollified and left quickly, not storming out but coming close. Outside the courthouse, he slammed his right fist into the palm of his left hand.

"John Ross is too old to deal with Watie. There must be another way!"

"I haven't had the pleasure of meeting your principal chief, and all I know is from watching, but he strikes me as a competent man. Not everything gets done by bullet and knife. I think John Ross knows that."

"He is a wise man," agreed Benjamin, "but he is old. His sons are not as capable, which is why he refuses to surrender power to them."

"What of that John Drew he sent out to deal with Watie?" Fargo was startled when Benjamin Threekiller

36

spat in response. The man stomped off which saying a word. Nor did he have to. He had expressed his opinion of Drew's competence eloquently.

"I need to poke around town and see if I can find what happened to the deputies," Fargo called after Ben. Fargo decided it was best to let the man stew a spell and get over his anger at what he saw as John Ross's cowardice. He turned slowly, looking all around them in a full circle.

"What's wrong?" asked Benjamin, stopping a few yards off and glaring at Fargo.

"Nothing. Maybe we ought to get back to your farm. I can find what I need later." Fargo mounted, keeping a sharp eye out for the rough-looking men who took more than a passing interest in him and Benjamin Threekiller. The men tried too hard to be nonchalant. They ended up sticking out like an apprentice carpenter's thumb. Fargo considered returning to the courthouse and enlisting John Ross's help, then discarded the notion. There was nothing illegal in watching others in the street. What could he accuse the men of doing?

"Can you ride fast?" Fargo asked.

"Why do you ask?"

"Might be nothing more than that crack I took to the head making me imagine things, but I don't think so." Fargo saw a half-dozen men come together, talk briefly, then ride as a group in the direction he and Benjamin took.

"They are Watie's men. I know it!" cried Benjamin.

"Then you ride like you mean it," Fargo said. "Let me handle them." He touched the six-shooter in its holster and glanced down at the Henry rifle in its saddle scabbard. He was armed and loaded for bear. Fargo put his heels into the Ovaro's flanks and sent the horse rocketing off. He caught up with Benjamin quickly, motioned for the older man to keep riding, then cut off the road and doubled back.

If the men in Tahlequah were on their heels, Fargo would spot them quickly—from their rear. That gave him a small advantage of surprise. It might be enough.

Fargo waited only a minute or two before the tight knot of riders trotted into view and passed where he hid amid a small stand of trees. He pulled his Henry from its sheath, levered in a round and took off after the horsemen.

They heard him the instant he got out onto the road. Wheeling about, the men fanned out as they faced him. Fargo estimated his chances and decided they were good. He already had his rifle out and could take down at least two of them if they went for their six-guns. The remaining three might open fire, but Fargo thought he was a better shot. And his horse didn't shy and get nervous when the lead began flying. He would have a more stable base to fire from than any of the Cherokees.

"Why are you gents following us?" Fargo called to see what response he could elicit.

"This is a free road. We can take it wherever we want."

"Then you won't mind waiting a spell," Fargo said, resting the rifle across his saddle in front of him.

"Why should we wait for you to tell us when to go? You're not Cherokee!"

"Nope, I'm not," Fargo said, choosing his words carefully. "What I am is in control of the situation. You followed us from town. Why'd you want to go and do a thing like that?"

The men exchanged looks and turned sullen. Fargo saw he wouldn't get a straight answer out of them, nor had he expected one. He played for time so Ben could get back to his farm safely.

Even as that thought crossed his mind, he heard rapid gunfire from farther down the road. The five Cherokees facing him looked at one another, then whooped loudly and rode off in different directions, leaving Fargo alone in the road.

Another gunshot echoed from down the road. Somehow, this one sounded Final. Deadly.

Fargo gave the Ovaro its head to gallop. The road dipped down and paralleled a small creek, then curved around through a stand of trees. Fargo reined back when he saw what lay in the road ahead. His heart almost exploded in anger when he jumped to the ground and knelt beside Benjamin Threekiller. It was as he thought.

The man was dead.

Fargo carefully examined the body. His anger grew to a white-hot rage. The first shots had caused Benjamin to slow and probably stop to see what trouble was ahead. This made him a sitting duck for a sniper who shot the man in the back. Fargo saw the single round had entered on the left side and had ripped through the defenseless man's heart, existing with a rush of life's blood out the front.

Fargo got to his feet, drew his Colt and began the hunt. He doubted he would find anything—and he was right. The spot where the sniper had lain in wait was obvious to him. Broken twigs, crushed leaves, even a scraped spot on top of a low tree limb where the killer had rested his rifle to steady his cowardly shot.

The men in the road had hooted and hollered and stopped Benjamin Threekiller to give an easy target. They had not even had the guts to shoot Threekiller facing him.

A cracking of a small, dry limb caught his attention. Fargo swung around, sharp eyes scanning the thicket. He saw a flash some distance away.

"Stop!" he called, although he knew the real killer would never do that. The man he chased lit out like his boots were on fire. Fargo wasted no time going after him. The thick undergrowth impeded his pursuit, tearing at the tough buckskin and holding him back as he struggled to close the distance.

Fargo lifted his six-shooter and fired when he caught the flash of a face ahead. He missed. If anything, the shot had the opposite reaction than the one he wanted. It added speed to the killer's retreat.

Twisting, turning furiously, he got free of the brambles and plunged out onto a game trail. His long legs pumped hard as he ran after the man who had murdered Ben. Fargo fired again when he saw the man across a clearing getting ready to mount a horse. If the killer got away now, Fargo might never find him.

He fired again, more to spook the horse than to stop the murderer. The horse bucked but the man—a Cherokee from his looks—held on and put his head down low as he urged the horse forward. He looked back once, giving Fargo the briefest glimpse of a coppery face sheened with sweat. Then he plunged ahead and vanished into the thick forest.

Fargo sucked in a lungful of air and ran full speed after Ben's fleeing slayer. The trail was easy to follow for a hundred yards. Then it vanished. The rider had crossed a rocky patch, dashed down to the creek and disappeared as surely as if he had gone up in a puff of smoke. He might be hiding nearby or he might be a mile away.

Benjamin Threekiller's assassin had escaped by knowing the terrain better than Fargo.

This cemented the idea that the bushwhacker was Cherokee and might even live in the area.

Pulling off burrs and jerking out a few thorns from his buckskins, Fargo returned to the place where Benjamin had been cut down. He whistled and his pinto trotted over from where it had been grazing contentedly. He wrestled Ben's body up and over the horse's rump before fastening it down with rawhide strips. When Fargo mounted, the doubled weight caused the Overo to whinny in protest.

"We'll be back in town soon enough," Fargo said, patting the horse's neck. The ride to Tahlequah was filled with a silent, festering anger.

Fargo dismounted in front of the courthouse, pulled Ben Threekiller from behind the saddle and hoisted the body over his shoulder. He mounted the steps amid total silence from onlookers and went directly to the room where John Ross still held his council.

Ross looked up. His dark eyes went wide, but he said nothing as Fargo dropped the body into a chair by the door.

"They gunned him down in an ambush not five miles outside your capital," Fargo said accusingly.

"You fought them?" Ross asked, looking at Fargo and pointedly ignoring the body slumped in his chair.

"Five of them—I think they were part of a gang—engaged me while at least two others stopped Benjamin. Then another one shot him in the back from hiding. I chased the killer, but he got away."

"You saw the man?"

Fargo described the murderer the best he could. Ross sat silently, his ancient visage giving no hint about the thoughts racing through his mind. He finally scowled a little, put his skeletal hands on the desk in front of him and levered himself to his feet.

"This is a bad thing. From your description, the man responsible might be one of Stand Watie's. Then again, perhaps he is not. There is no way to be sure since you did not see it with your own eyes."

"Find him and you might pick up a bloody trail leading back to this Watie," Fargo said.

"He is a powerful man with powerful friends in our nation," Ross said, choosing his words carefully. "I have wanted him stopped for a long time." A humorless smile came to the old man's thin lips. "Believe me when I say I have tried for years to stop him." He walked to the chair and laid his hand on Threekiller's head. "Go with the spirits, old friend," Ross said solemnly.

"That's it?" asked Fargo, outraged. "What about protecting his family from Watie? Have you forgotten your duty as principal chief to protect men like Threekiller?"

"No, I haven't," Ross said in a voice that sounded old and broken. "Rest assured we are doing all we can to stop such mayhem, whether caused by Watie or others. There are many within the Cherokee Nation who ignore the law. It is difficult to stop them all."

Fargo saw he wouldn't get any satisfaction from John Ross. He left the courthouse and headed back to the Threekiller farm to do the hardest chore possible: he had to tell Seth and Anna their father had been cruelly murdered.

5

"Seth is taking it hard," Anna said, dabbing at tears leaking from her own dark eyes. "I've never seen him like this."

"It's never easy learning that your father's been killed," Fargo said, carefully watching the lovely woman for any sign that he was upsetting her more. "Having him gunned down only makes it worse."

"Worse for Seth because he did nothing about it, he wasn't there, he should have been responsible for Father's safety." Anna looked hard at Fargo. More tears welled. "He is cursing himself doubly because *you* were there."

"I wish I had done more," Fargo said, "but it never occurred to me I was being decoyed. That doesn't set well with me," he said, a steely edge coming into his words. "It won't happen again."

"Skye, this is not your fight. You came into Indian Territory to find the men who killed your partner. You don't have to stay to fight this battle, too." Anna sniffed and tears flowed freely now.

"I don't have to," Fargo said, "but I'm going to. As bad as Coot's death was to bear, your father's is worse."

"Why?" she asked dabbing at her bloodshot eyes.

"Coot Marlowe was a bounty hunter. He lived to find the worst of the worst and expected to die every morning he got up. Your father was a farmer and shouldn't have had to live with the specter of death hovering at his elbow."

"He wasn't well," Anna said, as if this might excuse some of the guilt Fargo felt for letting Benjamin Three-

42

killer ride into an ambush. "He might not have lived out the year."

"Then that's a year of life he was cheated out of," Fargo said firmly. "Someone has to pay for it, and since Ross doesn't seem inclined to pursue the matter, I will."

"You don't belong here," came Seth's angry voice from the bedroom. Fargo turned to see the young man supporting himself in the doorway, more by force of will than his feeble grip on the doorjamb. "I can find Father's killer. Do as Anna said. Ride on. You have work of your own to do—outside Indian Territory."

"I never liked anyone telling me where I should be and where I shouldn't," Fargo said, holding his anger in check. Seth had just lost his father and had never cottoned much to Fargo or his ways of doing things. It might be that he knew Anna and Fargo had hit it off. Saving him from Watie's men had to rankle, too, making Seth feel less than capable.

"Get out," Seth said. "I'll see to it that John Ross gets a posse together and rides down the killers. They must be Watie's men. Who else would do such a thing?"

"Seth, please," Anna started. The young man angrily motioned her to silence.

"I saw the man who shot your father down. You didn't see him," Fargo said, knowing he would be hard-pressed in court to swear to the killer's identity. Not seeing him pull the trigger was a problem, but the brief glimpse of the man's face made it all the more difficult to testify with certainty and see that justice was done.

Fargo had to be completely convinced he had found the right man before he would drag him to Tahlequah for trial. But to do that meant nosing around Stand Watie's farm and checking out his men. Only after he had settled Benjamin Threekiller's murder could Fargo turn his attention back to finding the outlaws responsible for Coot's death.

"I can capture him! I'll kill him when I find him!" shouted Seth Threekiller.

"Please, Skye," said Anna, her hand warm on his arm. "Go now and let Seth cool off."

"I've got business to tend to," Fargo said.

"Let John Ross take care of it," called Seth. "He's the law in these parts. You're just an interloper!"

With those words ringing in his ears, Fargo left the Threekiller house and went to the barn. He hesitated when he came to the pile of straw where he and Anna had made love. She had nursed him back to health after he had been shot.

Gunned down like Benjamin Threekiller.

Fargo saddled his Ovaro and rode out, vowing not to get crushed between the two forces hammering Indian Territory. Stand Watie, with his men on one side, and John Ross, apparently with the reins of Cherokee government loosely held in his hands, would collide one of these days and more than a solitary farmer would get killed. Fargo didn't want to be there when that fight started.

But he would bring Benjamin Threekiller's murderer to justice.

Riding to the spot where Ben had been cut down, he studied the road and surrounding area until he found where the two riders had waited. These were the decoys, the men responsible for Benjamin stopping to give the real killer a good shot at his exposed back. Since Fargo had lost the killer's tracks in the woods, he decided to follow the trail left by these two men.

They did nothing to hide their hoofprints, making tracking easy for him. Maybe too easy. Fargo grew warier as he rode, wondering if he was being lured into a trap. Then he decided the riders had been overly confident. Who would track them?

Their trail led straight to the road leading to Stand Watie's house a few miles north of Tahlequah. Fargo squinted at the house about a quarter mile distant from the gate across the road and wondered if he ought to ride up and boldly ask for Benjamin's killer. From the way the tracks were jumbled at the gate, he could not prove the men he had trailed had entered.

For all that, he was assuming they even knew the killer. It made sense that they were in cahoots, but Fargo had no proof. He was acting on instinct—and that usually stood him in good stead.

Something about the gate and the distant house alerted him to what a mistake it would be to accost Watie without proof and a posse at his back. Fargo rode back and forth along the fence and saw how a pair of horses had skirted the farm recently. Fargo followed this path until it curved away from the fence and went down a slope toward a rapidly flowing stream.

He had no idea if he trailed Watie's men or just a pair of riders who had come in this direction. That doubt turned him more cautious. The last thing he wanted to do was make a false accusation that would enflame Watie and set off the war between the Cherokee factions.

Bringing a killer to justice was one thing, but triggering a civil war among the Cherokee was something else. For all he knew, the Five Civilized Tribes might take sides and ignite the entire of Indian Territory.

He had been in the saddle all day and needed to rest his horse. Fargo took the chance to let the Ovaro graze while he scouted on foot. He followed the stream until he heard boisterous voices a little ways uphill. Turning even more cautious, Fargo advanced and then went to his belly and wiggled forward until he got the campsite into view.

He was partially hidden by approaching dusk. The men in the camp did not see him because they weren't paying attention as they should have. They joked and jostled each other, moving around so Fargo eventually got a good look at all the men.

He did not recognize any of the five men as being among those he had braced just before Benjamin Threekiller was gunned down—but he did recognize the man he had chased through the woods. The Cherokee sat on a stump, mopping his face with a bandanna and looking uneasy. He spoke a few times to the others, all white, in the camp. They ignored him as they continued telling their bawdy jokes.

Fargo circled, coming up behind the Cherokee. The man was on edge, but not expecting Fargo's sudden

45

surge, the strong arm that circled his throat, or the way he was dragged back bodily into the twilight-lit undergrowth.

"You make a sound and it'll be your last," Fargo warned, his Arkansas toothpick at the man's throat. The Cherokee stared at him with wide eyes. Then the man turned panicky and heaved upward, throwing Fargo to one side.

"You!" the Cherokee cried, slithering away into the dusk. Fargo cursed the noise the man made but felt lucky that his quarry went away from the camp where the other four men might have helped.

Fargo pounced, landed on the man's back and bore him to the ground. Pushing the Cherokee's face into the ground cut off his cries. Fargo made sure his captive understood the situation by poking him with the thick knife blade.

"So you recognized me, eh?" Fargo said. "The only place you might have seen me before is when I chased you after you shot Ben Threekiller in the back." For a moment, the man went limp in surrender. Then he surged as if he had stepped into an anthill. The man fought like a trapped rat trying to throw off his captor, convincing Fargo that he had hit on the truth.

Using his knife, Fargo dug the tip deeper into the Cherokee's side. It would be easy and satisfying to plunge it in. Ben's death would be avenged, and John Ross wouldn't be bothered with holding a trial that might split his nation apart. But Fargo only probed a fraction of an inch before the man winced in pain and gave up.

"I don't know you. You try to kill me!"

"Tell it to John Ross," Fargo said, dragging the man to his feet. Thrusting the knife under the man's chin kept him quiet as they retraced Fargo's route. He stopped when he spotted the small corral with the men's horses.

"Get yours," Fargo ordered, watching closely as the man reluctantly obeyed. The Cherokee tried to spook the horse and distract Fargo, but the Trailsman was ready for an escape attempt. The other horses reared, neighed and ran off, but Fargo still had his prisoner. He grabbed both the Cherokee and the man's horse to prevent them from joining the others in their bid for freedom.

He shoved the Cherokee to the left side of his horse, then mounted behind him, knife still poking into the man's side. The first cut Fargo had inflicted bled sluggishly, probably more painful than serious. Fargo silently guided the Indian out of the camp as the other four men came running up to see what the ruckus was.

"Hey, they're stealin' our horses!" cried one. Bullets sang through the air but by the time the men reacted Fargo and the Cherokee were out of range.

Fargo drew his Colt and held it on Benjamin's killer as he mounted his Ovaro.

"What do you do with me?" demanded his prisoner.

"Back to Tahlequah. Now!"

It had taken most of the night to reach the Cherokee capital and the first dim streaks of dawn lit the sky in the direction of the Mississippi. Fargo felt a pang. Coot Marlowe was buried on the other side of that river and he had yet to find his killers. But Fargo was content for the moment in having found Benjamin Threekiller's bushwhacker.

The backshooter had ridden slowly, obviously waiting for any chance to escape that came his way. Fargo made sure none did. The Cherokee grew increasingly uneasy as they approached Tahlequah and certain judgment.

"You have wrong man. To you white eyes we all look alike."

"Maybe so," Fargo said, "but I saw you gun down Threekiller."

"No one saw me! I was hidden!"

Fargo nodded. He had been pretty sure he had the right man. Now he was positive.

"There's the courthouse." He gestured with his six-shooter and got the man into the lobby without any trouble.

"What's this?" cried an Indian sitting at the far side of the lobby.

"I want to see John Ross. I brought in Threekiller's bushwhacker."

"You have no right!" the man cried, thrusting out his chin belligerently. "You are not Cherokee! Or Creek or Cree. Or—"

"Hush, Mr. James," came John Ross's deep voice. He sounded stronger today and walked with a deliberate pace as he came from the office where Fargo had left Benjamin Threekiller's body.

"He is your pawn!"James cried, pointing at Fargo.

"He is no man's servant," Ross said. His eyes drifted to the man wincing every time Fargo poked the muzzle of his six-gun into his back. "Who is this?"

"Don't rightly know his name," Fargo admitted, "but he pulled the trigger on Benjamin Threekiller."

"You know this?"

"He confessed it," Fargo said.

"Why would any Cherokee tell a white man a thing like that?" demanded James.

"Who are you?" Fargo asked. "What's it to you?"

"He works for Stand Watie," Ross said, the words coming from his lips as if they were dipped in acid. "He works for Watie, and he will keep quiet because his chief asks him to."

"You are tearing apart the Cherokee Nation, Ross," James declared hotly. "Don't let this . . . bounty hunter . . . dictate law to you."

"This one will stand trial according to *our* law," Ross said, glaring at Watie's lieutenant as he put a hand on Fargo's prisoner. "If you have anything pertinent to say, you will be heard then."

James snorted like a bull ready to attack. He towered over the frail John Ross and made fists, but did not browbeat the Cherokee's principal chief. James stormed off, pausing at the door to point menacingly at Fargo and say, "Cherokee justice is for Cherokees. You have no part in it!"

James vanished into the new morning the threat hanging heavily.

6

Fargo steamed as he rode from Tahlequah. He knew nothing about the Cherokee who had warned him away from acting as a bounty hunter in Indian Territory other than that Ross had said he was one of Stand Watie's lieutenants. Nobody told the Trailsman where he could go and what he could do.

Still, Fargo had done his duty and brought in the man responsible for Benjamin Threekiller's death. He did not need to act as policeman for the entire Cherokee Nation. Let Ross and Watie hammer out their differences and try to achieve a semblance of peace in the area. Fargo had the feeling they faced as much danger from outside their nation as they did from within as long as the Osage and Comanche continued to prey upon their settlements in the west and the slavery situation churned and boiled in all the other directions around them in the United States.

Fargo forced the Indian concerns from his mind and concentrated on finding Mustang Jack McGhee and his murderous gang. The outlaws wouldn't parade around Tahlequah openly or they would create enough hatred that both Ross and Watie would combine forces to stop them. That meant McGhee did all his mischief across the Mississippi and came to Indian Territory to hide out and cause as few ripples around him as possible.

He chuckled when he thought that might be the best course of action for any white man traveling in this land. Don't be seen. Ride fast and never look back. But it was worth it if he succeeded in capturing Coot Marlowe's killer. Judge Ringo had put a considerable amount of trust in him and Fargo felt as if he was letting the judge down. As he turned his attention to figuring out where McGhee was most likely holed up, he couldn't help wondering what had happened to the deputies sent along with him. Delacroix and Thomas must have been killed.

That was his starting point. The area around the campsite where he had gotten buck fever must have two new graves—or at least picked-clean skeletons left by coyotes and buzzards. Either way, Fargo felt an obligation to let the judge know the fate of his two lawmen. They might have families that needed to be notified. Nothing was quite as bad as spending a lifetime wondering what had become of a loved one, even if Fargo found little to be considered lovable about either of the deputies.

He skirted the Threekiller farm and headed east, hunting for the spot where Seth Threekiller had found him. The terrain was hilly, and the lush, grassy vales had a certain sameness to them. A light fog hung over the deepest parts of the valley, making his search even more arduous. In spite of the difficulty of his search, Fargo felt more alive now than he had in weeks. His head wound was healed, and he rode without getting dizzy. And he was once more on the trail of the men responsible for killing his partner.

Fargo heard a stream gurgling in the valley before he saw it. He gave his Ovaro its head and reached the stream quickly. While the horse drank its fill, Fargo poked around and finally saw a distant hill with a distinctive lightning-struck tree atop it. This might be near the spot where McGhee and his gang had camped. It had the feel and details like the burned tree resonated with him.

On foot, Fargo started his search and found an old campsite within twenty minutes. He sifted through the dirt and turned over the ash in the firepit, hunting for any trace of the outlaws. Nothing. Another ten minutes of searching brought him to the spot where he had been gunned down. He turned in a full circle, then faced the camp.

"This is it," he said with certainty. He had ridden up on McGhee and then taken cover at this very spot. He even found the broken bushes where he had pitched facedown after being shot. Fargo tried to figure out where the sniper who shot him had been hiding, but couldn't. The best he could tell, the gunman had to have come from behind him.

Fargo remembered that the fight had started quickly, and it hardly seemed likely anyone from the camp could have circled around him that fast. Fargo shook off the inconsistencies and chalked it up to a member of the gang being out in the woods, possibly pursuing the same activity as Mustang Jack McGhee. They might have bought buckets of beer and needed to relieve themselves, or the unseen gunman might have been out hunting and found Fargo's back instead of a deer.

Fargo touched the wounded spot on his scalp. It would leave a long pink scar where the bullet had chipped out part of his skull, but otherwise he was none the worse for the experience—and he had been nursed back to health by Anna.

He hiked back to the empty camp and wondered how long it had been abandoned. A week or longer, from the look of the ground. For another man, this would have been a dead end. Not for Skye Fargo. He dropped to his belly and examined every square inch of the camp until he found old hoofprints cut into sod leading to the north. Getting his Ovaro, Fargo headed in that direction, following the bends and turns of the valley until it spilled out into flatter prairie country.

For three days Fargo rode looking for any trace of Mustang Jack McGhee. On the fourth day he found the outlaw's new camp by pure accident. A seldom-used road led Fargo to the north, and he spotted a dozen men camped on either side of the road. He reined back and studied them carefully, thinking the band was too large to be McGhee's road agents.

After a half hour of observation Fargo learned who the men were. A wagon rattled along the road and was stopped. From the way the armed men circled the wagon and poked through its contents, it was obvious they were

Stand Watie's men out to be sure nothing went across the prairie they did not approve first.

Rather than tangle with Watie's gunmen, Fargo turned to the west and rode in a wide circle. He had hardly gone two miles when he came across fresh tracks leading to a ravine. From the number, he surmised no fewer than five men had ridden here recently—and no more than eight. About the right size for McGhee's outlaw gang.

Fargo's heart leapt at his luck when he spotted two men patrolling the edge of the ravine before they saw him. With all his skill, he approached the ravine on foot and peered to the dry bottom. A slow smile crossed his face. Mustang Jack McGhee sat at the fire, pouring himself another cup of coffee, unaware anyone but his own gang was within miles.

Fargo guessed they had camped here to avoid Watie's men—or could the Cherokees better be called vigilantes? McGhee wouldn't have a chance against them if they took it into their heads that he was an interloper and opposed Watie's interests.

"Hey, Jack, how long do we have to patrol up here?" called a sentry. "I don't think them Indians are gonna come this way. They was too busy out on the road."

"You're prob'ly right," Mustang Jack said, "but you stay up there anyhow. Keep a sharp eye out. I didn't escape Arkansas to be strung up by a bunch of Cherokees."

The sentry grumbled and went back to his slow patrol along the lip of the ravine. Fargo watched until the man's head vanished. The sun was setting and long shadows marched across the floor of the ravine in the direction of McGhee's fire. A bold strike might capture the outlaw. Fargo pictured himself fading into that shadow and slowly crossing the sandy spit to reach the outlaw leader. A quick swing of his Colt would buffalo McGhee. Getting him out of camp would be dicier since there were two others nearby.

The challenge appealed to Fargo. He slipped to the far side of the ravine and crept forward in the shadow, taking advantage of depressions and rocks as he went to hide himself, but when he was within a dozen feet of

McGhee, the outlaw jumped to his feet and said, "It's time, boys. Let's ride."

"Think we can trust that stupid son of a bitch?" asked one man, hitching up his gun belt, then drawing his six-shooter and rolling the cylinder to be sure it was fully loaded.

"I don't know how he got himself caught, but he got away quick. That's what matters," McGhee said, checking his own six-gun. Fargo pressed himself as flat as he could on the ravine floor. The men all had their pistols drawn. If he was spotted now, he'd end up with more holes in him than a knotty pine board.

The men left their camp, mounted and rode up the ravine. Fargo cursed, slipped back and cautiously topped the rim of the ravine. The two sentries were also mounted and riding along. He dashed to where he had left his Ovaro, mounted and went after the outlaws in the fading sunlight.

Their voices carried on the wind blowing into their faces.

". . . supply wagon's just what we need," McGhee said.

"That's if Gallegina told us right. I dunno 'bout him, Jack. It sounded like he got caught for the killin' mighty easy."

"He hightailed it out of Tahlequah and has to play square with us. Who'd put up with him back there?" asked Mustang Jack McGhee. The outlaw leader laughed and added, "Besides, I can use some cannon fodder. Gallegina's just the one for that since there ain't nobody'd miss the fool."

The words were distant, muffled and possibly changed by the wind and night, but Fargo stiffened at the outlaw leader's words. He rode a little faster, daring more now to see who joined the gang.

"There he is," Mustang Jack said. "Hey, Gallegina!"

Fargo hung back as a dim, dark figure trotted over to McGhee.

"I told you to call me Buck," the one identified as Gallegina said. "I shun my Cherokee name. They are weak. I would be strong like you, Mustang Jack."

"What's wrong?" asked McGhee. "You weren't willing to ride with us before."

"But not too unwilling to take our money in exchange for information," drawled the road agent at McGhee's right hand. "Seems he throws in with whoever'll take him."

"Stand Watie would have let me be hanged for doing his work," Gallegina said. "I killed his enemy and he refused to save me from John Ross's jail. Your men, Ned and Lucas, helped me when I needed to kill Threekiller for Watie. Watie turned his back on me when I was caught. You did not."

"How'd you get nabbed?" asked McGhee.

"A white man," Gallegina said angrily. "But I escaped."

"So you want to throw in with us, the meanest, dirtiest, nastiest gang in all Indian Territory!" said McGhee's henchman, laughing at the Cherokee. "It'll take more than shooting down a man to get in with us."

Fargo went cold when he heard the byplay. The Indian he had captured and turned over to John Ross for trial was now asking to join McGhee's gang. He had to face the choice of either recapturing Ben's murderer or bringing in Mustang Jack McGhee.

For Anna or to avenge the memory of his dead partner? Which way did he choose? There were too many killers on the loose within the borders of the Cherokee Nation.

Fargo discarded the wild idea he could take both men back. McGhee rode with four alert, well-armed road agents as bodyguards. Recapturing Gallegina might be easier, but where should Fargo deposit him this time? With the cavalry at Fort Gibson? John Ross had shown little skill or resolution holding Gallegina for Ben's murder.

At least he knew where he had to take Mustang Jack McGhee. Judge Ringo was not the kind to let him go once he had been locked up.

Fargo trailed the gang, deciding his only chance was to see which way the wind of chance blew and go with it. If he could capture McGhee and get away, he would. Similarly, if his only chance was to retake Gallegina, Fargo would do that and come back later for McGhee.

The twilight turned into inky darkness that made riding difficult. Fargo kept the men's silhouettes against the horizon in view. None of them bothered to look back, allowing him to close the distance between them. He was still undecided about which of the murderers to go after when McGhee lifted his hand and stopped his men.

"There's the supply wagon," Gallegina said. "As I promised."

"Sure enough," McGhee said. "Who's it belong to?"

"Does it matter?"

"We don't want Watie madder at us than necessary. His men patrol this entire range around Cowskin Prairie. It wouldn't do if he ran us off, and we had to go back into Arkansas."

"Better to go north into Kansas," said McGhee's henchman. "There's not much worth stealin' up north, but an empty belly's better than a stretched neck."

"You're right about that, Ned," responded McGhee. Fargo tensed. He had been warned about Ned Sondergard, McGhee's right-hand man. He had found the entire pit of vipers.

"So, Buck," said McGhee with a hint of sarcasm at the Indian's choice of summer name, "whose goods are we appropriating for our own use?"

"A merchant in Muskogee," Gallegina said with ill grace. "I do not like him, either."

"You got a powerful hate for all your redskin brothers, don't you?" asked Ned Sondergard.

"Enough of that, Ned," McGhee said sharply. "You circle and come up on them from behind. Take Buck with you. The rest of us will ride on up and see if they're hospitable."

"I won't let any of 'em escape," Sondergard promised. He and Gallegina rode off, a stony silence settling between them.

Fargo knew that he couldn't pluck McGhee from the middle of the other three men without a lot of gunplay so he reluctantly abandoned his hope of capturing Coot Marlowe's murderer and went after Gallegina and Sondergard.

As guilty as Sondergard likely was of unspecified crimes while riding with Mustang Jack McGhee, Fargo was willing to let him ride away in exchange for hogtying Gallegina. He had found McGhee once. He could run him down again.

The teamsters out on the prairie had not bothered to post a guard. Whether they felt safe from, or perhaps protected by, Stand Watie's men, Fargo did not know. He saw McGhee and the three road agents with him ride up boldly and engage the men with the supply train in conversation to be certain they were not walking into a trap.

When McGhee whipped out his six-shooter, Fargo knew he had to act. He galloped after Gallegina and Sondergard. He cursed his bad luck when he thought he had lost sight of them. Then he spotted two riders ahead, a bit more to the north than he expected.

Fargo veered and curved away from the teamsters and their problems with McGhee. It pained him that the freighters would be robbed and maybe killed, but he couldn't stop the entire gang singlehandedly. After he returned Gallegina to jail, he could lead the cavalry detachment out of Fort Gibson and track down McGhee and his men, if necessary. Robbing a supply wagon ought to be enough to arouse the cavalry's ire.

Unexpected gunfire raked past him. Fargo ducked low and drew his six-shooter. Sucking in a deep breath, he galloped hard, heading straight for Sondergard and Gallegina. They must have spotted him and opened fire, thinking he rode guard for the freighters. Or maybe they took shots at anyone, just for fun. Fargo wondered anew how he had misjudged where they would be riding. They ought to have been much closer to the wagon than this.

He kept low and closed the distance between them. He held his fire until he came within range. Fargo lifted his six-shooter, cocked it and started to fire. At the last instant he jerked the pistol skyward and called out in surprise, "Delacroix! Thomas! It's me, Fargo!"

He had found the two deputies—at the worst possible time. Their shots had alerted Sondergard and Gallegina, sending them racing for the teamsters' wagon to warn McGhee.

7

"Stop shooting!" cried Fargo, his grip tightening on the handle of his six-shooter. He did not want to shoot the two lawmen but had to keep them from upsetting the applecart. Or was it too late already?

Fargo twisted in the saddle and listened hard to the pounding hooves heading for the teamsters' wagon. Gallegina yelled at the top of his lungs and from the sudden gunfire, Fargo knew that McGhee had answered by cutting down the freighters.

"You killed them by shooting like that," Fargo accused as Delacroix and Thomas rode up. Both men held their smoking six-guns as if they would use them on him. "It's me. Fargo!" His anger knew no bounds. He had been tossed on the horns of the dilemma of which killer to go after and had chosen Gallegina. Now his chances of capturing either Gallegina or McGhee had turned to dust.

"What are you goin' on about?" drawled Thomas. "For all that, how come you're still alive and kickin'?"

"Save the talk for later. That's McGhee robbing the freighters. He's got his entire gang with him, and we can catch them."

"How many?" asked Delacroix, obviously wary of the prospect of fighting too many outlaws.

"Five or six. What's the difference? They're killing innocent men to rob a supply wagon!" Fargo didn't wait to see if the two deputies followed. He wheeled his Ovaro around and galloped recklessly for the wagon. Lead sang through the night in his direction. He ignored it and plunged on. When he got within a dozen yards of the teamsters' wagon, he opened fire on the men working to unload supplies from the rear of the wagon. One of his slugs tore an inch-long groove in the wood side. Another took off an outlaw's hat.

Then Fargo was driven back by the heavy return fire. All the road agents opened fire on him at the same time. Barely escaping, he hit the ground some distance from the camp and checked himself for holes. He was wound up tighter than a two-dollar watch and knew he could have been winged and not have noticed. His quick examination showed he was still intact. He looked over his Ovaro and found the horse had miraculously escaped unhurt, too.

Fargo pulled his Henry from its sheath and started back on foot.

"What's going on?" demanded Delacroix, riding up more slowly. The deputy still had his six-shooter out but didn't aim it in Fargo's direction now.

"I told you. McGhee's gang is robbing the wagon. From what I saw, they slaughtered the driver and two others and are getting away with some of the supplies in the wagon. If I hadn't ridden up when I did, they'd have driven the wagon off and nobody would ever have known what happened to the teamsters."

"Mustang Jack McGhee?" asked Thomas, looking skeptical.

"Who else?" Fargo said, tired of such bullheaded refusal to believe him. He set off, keeping low and approaching the wagon from the side. This time he saw only unmoving bodies. The outlaws had ransacked the cargo, gotten some into their saddlebags and hightailed it, leaving behind only carnage.

Fargo poked one freighter with his rifle to check for life. He need not have bothered. Fargo looked up when Delacroix and Thomas rode into the death camp.

"You weren't shuckin' when you said they was dead," Thomas said, looking around. He shoved his six-gun into its holster and dismounted.

"We have to go after McGhee. I want him and a Cherokee named Gallegina."

"Why is that? What is this man to you?" asked Delacroix. The Cajun deputy remained in the saddle, his dark eyes fixed on Fargo.

"Gallegina killed Benjamin Threekiller, then escaped from the Tahlequah jail. He's thrown in with McGhee. He knows the territory, making him invaluable to McGhee."

"Reckon McGhee knowed 'bout all there was to know of Indian Territory to start with," Thomas said. "That's why he's so damned hard to run down. Don't see that any Injun joining up with him makes him that much more dangerous."

"They're both killers," Fargo said doggedly, checking the other two men. Both had been shot in the back of the head. Seeing their mortal wounds, Fargo reached up and touched his own skull. A tremor of pain quaked through his head and then faded like a bad dream.

"Our first chore's to get their remains buried, 'less you think it's more Christian to take 'em into Tahlequah so their people can be told what happened." Thomas walked around the small camp, poking through the dead men's belongings. Fargo had the image of a vulture swooping down to feast. Thomas saw his look and smiled insincerely, adding, "Thought it might be possible to identify 'em from their belongings. We could bury 'em straight away and not cart them into town."

"What happened when we found McGhee the first time?" Fargo asked. He touched the wound on his head again.

"We thought you were dead. One of the outlaws took a shot at you, you grabbed your head and then keeled over. Me and Delacroix thought you were dead, so we shot it out with the gang."

"They got away," guessed Fargo.

"They had position and a powerful lot more firepower than we did," Thomas said. "Livin' to fight another day seemed . . . prudent."

"So you left me for dead?"

Delacroix coughed nervously and looked as if he wanted to be anywhere else. "Look, Fargo, no offense to you. We thought you were dead, all stretched out and bloody. If it gets back to Judge Ringo that we lit out like we did, he's going to take away our badges." Delacroix still had his six-gun out and Fargo imagined it swinging in his direction. Fargo put his back against the wagon and levered a round into the Henry. The metallic *click-click* sounded like the peal of doom in the still night air.

"We may not be the best lawmen ever to pin on badges, but we try to do what we kin," Thomas said. "That's more 'n most of 'em workin' for Judge Ringo kin say."

"I want McGhee brought to trial for killing my partner. And I want Gallegina turned over to the Cherokee authorities for backshooting Benjamin Threekiller."

"You got a fixation about avenging this Indian fellow?" asked Delacroix, still looking as if he might make a move on Fargo.

"I feel responsible," Fargo said, not relaxing his vigilance for even an instant.

"Might be we can find this Gallegina and get him back where he belongs," said Thomas, finishing his search of the dead men's possessions. "Hard to go after McGhee at the same time, though."

"I can capture him again," Fargo said, his anger smoldering and threatening to burst into red-hot flame. The two lawmen were diverting him from the real mission of taking Jack McGhee back to Fort Smith by dangling Gallegina in front of him as a better target.

"Well, you know best," Thomas said, beginning to pick through the remaining contents of the wagon. "You gonna git on the trail or you want to wait for us?"

Fargo didn't bother answering. He left the two deputies to the chore of dealing with the bodies and returned to his Ovaro. Fargo jumped into the saddle and savagely slammed his rifle back into the sheath. The horse snorted and began crow-hopping. Fargo gentled the horse and then forced himself to calm down. It wasn't like him to lose his temper like that, but the two lawmen had managed to turn irritation into outright animosity toward them.

He touched the wound on his head again, trying to remember what had really happened when he had gone after McGhee. Someone had shot him from behind, and he had to wonder if it had been one of the outlaws, as the deputies claimed. They might have shot him by accident.

Or maybe it had not been an accident.

Gritting his teeth, Fargo rode into the night to find the trail left by the fleeing road agents. It took him the better part of an hour before he found fresh droppings to positively point out the trail. A quarter moon rose to light the path better for him. It was this silvery light that saved his life.

A glint amid some brush ahead along the trail drew his attention. Then Fargo saw the dark length of a rifle poking out. He flung himself to one side as the bullet raced through the space where he had been only a fraction of a second earlier. Kicking hard, Fargo got his right foot free of the stirrup as the Ovaro reared and pawed at the air.

A second shot went wide. By this time Fargo was advancing fast on the hidden sniper. Before, the outlaws had tried to shoot him in the back. He wondered why they changed their tactics now.

Fargo snorted. Buck fever. The urge to be rid of him. That he followed them might have spooked them even more. Fargo hit the ground hard and wiggled forward, his six-shooter shoved in front of him. He waited a moment, hunted for the sniper, then got his feet under him and charged with a loud shout.

He hit the patch of brush where the ambusher had crouched and crashed past. Fargo swung around, hunting for a target. Whoever had tried to gun him down had fired twice, then hightailed it. Fargo whistled and his pinto trotted to him. With a small jump, he was in the saddle and riding, alert for any sight or sound that would betray the would-be killer.

Sounds to his left, distant but growing louder, drew him. He knew he might be riding smack into the McGhee gang, but did not care. He was mad enough to fight a wildcat. Nobody killed two men he counted as friends and then tried to kill him—twice—and got away with it.

Fargo rode forward, then slowed when he heard loud voices. Half spoke in Cherokee. The replies were sometimes in English, sometimes not. As far as he knew, Gallegina was the only Indian riding with McGhee. The constant argument in the Cherokee tongue warned him he might not have found the outlaws, after all.

Heading for a deep ravine cut into the prairie, Fargo urged his horse down into it and waited, hidden by the embankment as the riders passed along the rim a few yards away.

Fargo sucked in his breath when he saw them. The men wore bandoliers like Mexican bandidos and carried at least two six-guns shoved into their belts. More than one rode with a shotgun resting in the crook of his arm, ready for immediate fighting. They passed Fargo's hiding place, riding across the moonlit prairie on their lookout for anyone who did not belong.

Only when they had vanished did Fargo let out his breath. He had almost been caught by what had to be one of Stand Watie's patrols. From the way they were armed, they were ready to fight a small war—or a big one. Nowhere in the group had Fargo spotted Gallegina or any of the outlaws riding with McGhee.

He considered the chance that a Watie-supporter had tried to ambush him, then discarded it. There was no need for them to shoot a man like that. They rode with the arrogance of men in charge, men who commanded as far as the distant horizon. If they had wanted him dead, they would have ridden up to him and simply shot him. Or chased him down and shot him. Watie's sentries had no reason to pussyfoot around, especially on Cowskin Prairie where Watie had a sprawling farm.

After biding his time to be sure the Cherokees were long past spotting him, Fargo tried to find the trail of the ambusher. Or McGhee's gang. He worried now that the tracks he had found earlier belonged to Watie's patrol rather than the road agents. The prairie was a desolate, deserted place and he had not thought to find more than one band of men riding together. From the large numbers he had spotted just tonight, Fargo knew he was dead wrong on that score.

Freighters, sentries, outlaws, even the two deputies had all been out roving across the grasslands. It was busier than downtown St. Louis, and Fargo wanted to put it all behind him as fast as he could. To do that meant he had to find Gallegina and McGhee and turn them over to the proper authorities without further delay.

He rode back and forth across a wide section of the prairie until he found tracks heading in the direction he had originally taken—and thought McGhee had gone. As he rode, he chewed on all that had happened to him. He didn't much like any of it, except meeting Anna, and even that now carried a bittersweet feeling. He could see how special her father had been to her, and now he was gone, dead at the hands of a cowardly backshooter that John Ross couldn't keep locked up.

Fargo was keyed up and jumped when a gunshot rang out, rolling like thunder over the quiet prairie. He put his heels to his Ovaro's flanks and raced ahead, homing in on the sound. The prairie had begun to lift and fall, trying to turn into hills and not quite making it. When Fargo topped a small rise, he stared down into a long, twisting section of land where foot-long tongues of flame licked out, first from the left and then from the right. From the position of the muzzle flashes, Fargo saw that two men were shooting at one who was fighting from the ground near a pile of rocks hardly larger than gravel-sized.

Two against one. Fargo figured the chances were good that the two men belonged to McGhee's gang and had come across a solitary traveler. He angled out and then curved back to come up behind the solitary gunman. From the sharp reports, the man used a rifle and the other two used six-shooters. A chill ran the length of his spine as he wondered if the man he sought to aid might have been the sniper who had almost cost him his life less than an hour earlier.

Fargo rode up, drew his six-gun and jumped to the ground. He didn't want a stray bullet hitting his horse. He made his way through the piles of rock and came out behind the lone gunman just as his rifle jammed.

"Hold it!" Fargo called. He wanted to get facts straight before he shot at or helped the man struggling to clean the jam in his rifle. The man, hidden in shadow, turned toward him as his two attackers swarmed over the top of the rocky piles.

"Stop!" Fargo shouted. "It's me. Fargo!" All three men responded.

"We got him, Fargo. We got the man who tried to ambush you," shouted Delacroix. Beside him Deputy Thomas aimed his six-gun directly at Seth Threekiller.

"Don't shoot!" Fargo repeated. "I know him."

Seth stood up, looking confused. Fargo matched him but did not let it show.

"What's going on?" Fargo demanded.

"We run him to ground," Thomas said. "He shot at you, then lit out like a scalded dog. Took us this long to run him down."

"I don't know what they're talking about," protested Seth. "I came out to find Gallegina and kill him. They attacked me."

"Let's just shoot him and get it over with," Delacroix said. "You said he escaped from the Tahlequah jail before."

"He didn't murder Benjamin Threekiller," Fargo said loudly to keep the deputies from pulling the triggers on their six-guns. "This is Benjamin's son!"

"Why'd he try to shoot you, then?" asked Thomas.

Fargo looked at Seth and wondered if the young man blamed him for his father's death enough to kill him. The sniper had used a rifle and Seth carried a rifle that still smoked from rapid firing.

"I didn't do anything. You believe me, don't you, Fargo?" Seth turned anguished eyes on him, but Fargo didn't know what to think. Someone had shot at him and then ridden in this direction. It seemed too much of a coincidence that the lawmen would find Seth Threekiller so quickly after the ambush.

Fargo shook his head and both deputies grinned ghoulishly as they raised their six-shooters.

8

"Try to shoot him and you'll get a bullet in your belly first," Fargo said coldly, turning to face Delacroix squarely. He figured the Cajun lawman was the leader of the pair. Thomas went along with whatever his partner said.

"Why'd you want to go do a thing like that?" asked Delacroix, his eyes sharp and focused on Fargo.

"I don't think he shot at me. No matter the way it looks," Fargo added lamely. The truth was that he could not say if Seth Threekiller had tried to shoot him. The man had a rifle and the deputies seemed to have cornered him. They claimed he had shot at Fargo. That made it their word against Seth's. Fargo wasn't sure who to believe.

"We have to get after McGhee," Thomas said. "Lollygaggin' here ain't doin' it for us."

"I say we turn this little fry over to the local authorities," Delacroix said. His words were logical, but Fargo felt he was being challenged again.

"Tahlequah's a long ways off," he said.

"Tahlequah? Why ride that far? Stand Watie's the man in charge up here on the prairie. Or had you not heard?"

"Watie'll kill me outright! My father and I both support John Ross." Seth turned forlornly to Fargo, then sagged. He looked as if he had accepted his death.

"I'll take him back to Tahlequah. You two can keep on McGhee's trail. He's out here somewhere and likely to be moving slower now that he's loaded down with loot from the wagon." Fargo turned bitter, thinking how close he had come to capturing Gallegina and possibly even Mustang Jack McGhee. If it had not been for the two Arkansas deputies he would have succeeded.

"We can ride together in that direction," Delacroix said. "Who knows what we might find, eh?"

"Fargo, I didn't shoot at you. I'm telling the truth!" cried Seth.

"Onto your horse," Thomas said. "Move your ass, or I'll shoot it full of holes to get you movin'." The deputy laughed harshly at the prospect of firing his six-shooter.

Seth mounted his horse. Fargo joined the two deputies and their prisoner, worried Delacroix and Thomas might gun down Seth while he fetched his horse. The pair argued in low tones and quickly fell silent when Fargo rode up.

Seth started to speak, but Thomas made a slow slashing motion with his finger across his throat warning the young man to stay quiet—or else.

"That way," Delacroix said, pointing across the inky-dark prairie. Fargo glanced at the sky and wondered how Delacroix could be so sure. Thin clouds had covered the sky, not promising rain but thick enough to blot out the stars and wan moon.

Fargo rode beside Seth but said nothing to him. The young man sweat like a pig, showing how nervous he was at the prospect of being captured by the two lawmen. Fargo did nothing to relieve his anxiety because he worried a mite about his own back. He kept to one side, making it more difficult for either of the deputies to shoot him, if they took it into their heads.

"Halt! Who goes there?" came the loud cry. Fargo's hand flashed to his Colt, then he froze. Ahead in the road were three riders, all armed with leveled shotguns. He twisted in the saddle and looked at the back trail. Four more men closed in behind them like bread around meat in a sandwich. He shoved his Colt back into its holster when he heard riders coming from both flanks. They were surrounded by enough firepower to reduce them to bloody tatters if they resisted.

"We are deputies hailing from Fort Smith across the

river," Delacroix said calmly. "We have a prisoner in custody we're taking in to Tahlequah."

"What's his crime?"

"He tried to shoot down this gent. That there's Skye Fargo, and he's riding with us." Thomas sounded as calm as his partner, as if they had expected to be stopped and had their stories ready. Fargo shook his head. What the two deputies said was nothing but the pure truth. They were not telling stories—they were simply telling what had actually happened.

If Fargo expected any reaction from the riders to the way Delacroix used his name, he was disappointed. Sometimes it opened doors. This time the Trailsman's name fell on deaf ears.

"Attempted murder's a crime we don't allow to pass. That's almost as bad as horse stealing." The leader of the vigilantes spoke rapidly to others in his band, the Cherokee flowing too fast for Fargo to catch even a single word. "We'll take him to Stand Watie."

"No!" cried Seth. The young man started to make a run for it, but Fargo reached out and grabbed at the reins of his horse, forcing it to wheel about. Seth's horse protested loudly as it turned in a tight circle rather than racing pell-mell across the prairie.

"I won't let anything happen to you," Fargo said quietly. Seth looked at him with equal parts of fear and skepticism but stopped trying to run.

"That is the proper thing to do," Delacroix said almost cheerily. He waved to Watie's men to come closer. The circle around Fargo and the others tightened like a noose around his neck.

"Lead the way," Fargo said.

"We'll go to Watie's farm. It's not five miles off," the leader of the vigilantes said. He motioned with his shotgun and got the tight knot of riders moving across the prairie. Now and then the moon came out and cast a silvery, eerie shroud on the ground. Fargo rode in silence, putting together all his arguments for when he was face-to-face with Stand Watie.

They reached the modest farmhouse. Fargo wasn't

sure what he had expected, but something grander would have suited a man intent on taking over the entire Cherokee Nation. The house was hardly larger than the Threekiller's, but was as neatly kept. The front door opened, silhouetting a large man in pale yellow light. He stepped out onto the porch and leaned against the railing.

"What've you brought now, William? Some of Ross's spies?"

"Nothing like that, Stand," the leader of the band said. He rode over and spoke rapidly with Stand Watie for several minutes. Then Watie nodded and motioned for Fargo and the others to ride closer.

"My good friend William Adair says this one's a killer."

"I was shot at. He didn't kill me," Fargo said before he thought.

"I didn't shoot at him!" shouted Seth.

"He's right. I don't know who shot at me."

"He's the one, Chief," Delacroix spoke up. "We're lawmen from Fort Smith come to hunt down a white man taking refuge in Indian Territory. We came across him as he was shooting at our friend Skye Fargo."

"I didn't—"

"Quiet," Watie said. He did not raise his voice but the command was obeyed immediately. "This has the look of a can of worms to me. You can't say if he shot at you?" Watie stared straight at Fargo.

"I cannot."

"But these deputies do?"

"We both do," chimed in Thomas.

"You have no authority to roam around my land," Watie said coldly. "But I recognize this one as Benjamin Threekiller's boy, Seth. He's always had a hot head and a sharp tongue."

"I didn't do anything," Seth protested.

"Since Chief Ross isn't inclined to enforce the law in the Cherokee Nation, I have to. That's why William and the others patrol my land—and protect all Cherokees from Jayhawker raids."

"And outlaws?" asked Fargo.

"We have had some trouble with them, but my sights are set on Chief Ross." Stand Watie spoke as if the man's name burned his tongue.

"What are you going to do with me?" asked Seth.

Watie looked at him, pursed his lips, then said. "There is a disagreement between these self-proclaimed lawmen and Skye Fargo. Since he is the aggrieved party, I would hear his thoughts."

"Let Seth go. He wasn't the one who ambushed me," Fargo said without hesitation.

"And *we* say this owlhoot tried to gun down Fargo," Delacroix said belligerently.

"Such disputed matters must be settled in a trial where all facts can be discussed fully." Watie turned to Fargo and told him, "You have one week to find someone who will confess to your attempted murder. If you are not back here by then with compelling evidence, Seth Three-killer will go before the Southern Rights Party tribunal for judgment."

"They're all slaveholders," cried Seth. "They'll hang me, no matter what."

"Hush," Fargo said. He had listened hard to what Stand Watie said and the way he said it. There was real disagreement—even bad blood—between Watie and Ross, but Stand Watie struck him as an honorable man. If he vouched for Seth's safety, Seth was as safe as if he were a babe in his mother's arms.

For a week.

"All right," Fargo said. He held up his hand to check Seth's angry outburst. Arguing now accomplished nothing but wasting precious time. Fargo had an idea who the ambushers were from the way both Delacroix and Thomas looked as if they had bitten into a green persimmon. How he could prove the two deputies were responsible was beyond him, but he had to try, or put up one hell of an argument in the Cherokee kangaroo court. Somehow, Fargo doubted anyone this side of Daniel Webster was eloquent enough a speaker to save Seth Threekiller in that event.

"We got business, Fargo," Thomas said. "Remember.

Judge Ringo sent us into Indian Territory to capture Mustang Jack."

Before Fargo could say a word, gunshots rang out. Stand Watie reached for a rifle and motioned to William Adair to take charge of Seth. For a fleeting instant, Fargo considered rescuing the young man. Then he put it out of his mind. Adair and a half dozen of Watie's vigilantes circled Seth, cutting him off. The rest of the men turned toward the source of the ruckus.

A lone rider came galloping up the road to Watie's front door. The man's horse was lathered, its eyes ringed in white and its rider waving a six-shooter around. As the rider neared, Fargo saw the rider was a very young man barely in his teens. He continued to cock and fire the six-gun, although it had long since been emptied.

"Father, Father!" the teenager cried. He jerked back on the reins and his horse dug its heels into the dirt, kicking up a small dust storm. Fargo saw the rider was Cherokee.

"Whoa, there, Saladin. Ease back and tell me what's got you so stirred up."

Fargo turned and looked to William Adair. Adair whispered, "Watie's oldest boy."

This made Fargo perk up his ears even more. Anything Saladin Watie said was likely to be taken as the gospel truth by his father.

Gasping for breath, Saladin said, "Raiders. Father, raiders hit Uncle Elias's farm. Shot it up."

"To your horses!" shouted Watie, vaulting over the railing and hitting the ground running. He and most of his men rushed to the corral to get their horses.

"Well, Fargo?" asked Delacroix. "Do you want to see what the hullabaloo is about?"

Fargo did, because the two deputies did. He turned his Ovaro's face and rode behind the two lawmen as they joined Watie's posse.

9

Fargo had expected to ride all night long but was surprised to find that the outlaws shooting up the farmhouse belonging to Stand Watie's brother were less than ten miles off. During the entire ride, Saladin Watie chattered like a magpie to his father, and Fargo watched the two deputies like a hawk. Delacroix and Thomas rode easily, as if they didn't have a care in the world.

While he might be wrong about them, Fargo had a feeling deep in his gut that told him the two lawmen were crookeder than a dog's hind leg. But he needed proof, both for Stand Watie and Judge Ringo, before he dared blame them. There was little Fargo disliked more than wild, baseless accusations. Prove it, then lock the pair up.

If they were guilty of half of what Fargo thought, they would swing.

He cocked his head to one side when he heard distant gunfire. His heart raced and he put his heels to the Ovaro's flanks to get it trotting. The rest of Watie's men had also heard the shots and responded as Fargo had.

"Be careful, men," Watie called. "We're likely facing men who'll kill and take some pleasure in it."

"We have to save Uncle Elias," Saladin said.

"For Elias!" went up the cry. Then the Cherokees scattered and rode toward the farmhouse with no battle plan. Fargo thought that was a good way to get killed, but said nothing. This was Stand Watie's attack, not his.

Fargo saw Watie and his son gallop off, six-guns clutched tightly in their hands. He looked around and saw that Delacroix and Thomas had slipped off and were riding away from the farm and the fight going on there. Fargo felt himself torn between adding his gun to Watie's attack and following the two deputies. They rode as if they knew where they were going.

The decision was hard, but Fargo made it. Watie had enough men to take on a dozen raiders. One more man on his side wouldn't turn the tide, should the battle go against him. But trailing the two lawmen might prove more enlightening. Even if they weren't riding to join the outlaws, Delacroix and Thomas held the key to freeing Seth Threekiller. Fargo owed it to the young man to clear his name.

One dead Threekiller was enough.

The fierce gunfight at the farm raged on, but the sounds faded as Fargo rode after the deputies. Delacroix and Thomas slowed and eventually stopped on top of a hill to look around and get their bearings. Fargo hid the best he could because the lawmen were studying their back trail to be sure no one followed them. After almost five minutes, the pair decided they were safe and rode on. Fargo took out after them, wanting to narrow their lead so he could get some solid evidence against them.

As Fargo topped the hill where the two deputies had stopped to reconnoiter, he heard the dull thudding of horses' hooves coming up from behind him. As Delacroix and Thomas had done, Fargo looked behind him on his back trail. The difference was that the lawmen had not seen him. Fargo spotted two men running their horses into the ground as they galloped long past their mounts' endurance.

Fargo eased his Colt from its holster and waited for the men to top the rise. As they did, he knew they wouldn't be riding off if they spotted him. Their horses were stumbling from exhaustion. Another dozen yards at a gallop would leave both animals dead.

"We made it," called the lead rider.

"Damn, but them Injuns sure put up a fight. And when the others showed up, we lit out. There's no way we coulda fought all of them," added the second rider.

Fargo wondered who they thought he was. He decided to find out.

"Where's McGhee?" he called, thinking this was a question the outlaws would respond to most readily. He had not anticipated McGhee's plan for attack or retreat.

"You ain't Mustang Jack!" cried the lead rider. He fired at Fargo, missing by several feet. Fargo kept his Ovaro under control. He stood a better chance if he remained still and forced the man to aim than if he danced around and walked into one of the wild shots.

"Where is he?" Fargo shouted. "Where's Mustang Jack?"

If he had any hope this would soothe the fears of the two outlaws, he was wrong. They both opened fire on him, forcing him to duck. Fargo let them fire until he was sure both men's six-shooters were empty. Then he trotted toward them.

"Give up. I've got you fair and square," he said loudly. The two men turned their horses and started back downhill.

As Fargo had figured, the horses were already past their limits of endurance. One stumbled and tossed its rider head over heels. The other horse reached the bottom of the gentle slope and then simply collapsed, dead before it hit the ground. Its powerful heart had likely burst from exhaustion.

Fargo took out his lariat and spun it a couple times, then rode forward in time to drop the hemp loop over the shoulders of the first road agent. With a sharp yank, he tightened the rope and pulled the man off his feet. Fargo rode down the hill to where the other man fought to get his trapped leg out from under his dead horse.

"Don't make it worse for yourself," Fargo said. He looped his end of the lariat around his saddle horn and jumped to the ground. Every time the lassoed outlaw tried to free himself, the Ovaro backed up and kept the line taut.

Seeing that the crook he had already captured wasn't going anywhere, Fargo turned his attention to the one caught under his dead horse. He held down his bile at the thought of the man running the poor horse into the ground like this. But then the outlaw rode with a gang inclined to shoot men in the back. For all Fargo knew, he had caught the very man who had gunned him down when he had first tried to arrest Mustang Jack McGhee.

"Don't—" Fargo did not get to finish his sentence before the man freed himself, leaving his boot trapped under the horse's weight. The owlhoot flopped around and somehow came up with his rifle.

Fargo dived to the side as the outlaw levered a round into the chamber and fired wildly. Fargo got to his knees and pulled out his six-shooter, but he didn't have a target. The road agent had run off, seeking refuge in a stand of trees a dozen yards away. He hobbled as he ran, handicapped by the missing boot, but fear lent speed to his awkward departure.

Slamming his pistol back into his holster, Fargo set off after the fleeing outlaw. He got into the wooded area and turned cautious. He didn't hear the man crashing through the copse ahead of him. Fargo remembered that the man was armed now with a rifle—and he felt unseen sights centering on him as had happened before.

Fargo ducked down, cut to his right and began to circle with the intent of coming out behind the highwayman if he laid in wait directly ahead. He had not gone ten yards when he spotted the outlaw flat on his belly and aiming toward the spot where Fargo would have appeared, had not instinct alerted him to the danger.

The soft whisper of metal moving across leather warned the gunman of something amiss with his plan. He came to his knees, ready to fire, but had no target.

"You're a dead man if you don't drop the rifle," Fargo told him. He aimed his Colt directly in the middle of the dark blotch that was the outlaw's body. A single shot might not kill him outright, but it would certainly put him into a world of hurt.

"Who are you? What do you want? We're just innocent cowboys. You can't—"

"Save it for Judge Ringo," Fargo said.

"You're the law!"

"From Fort Smith," Fargo said. "And you haven't dropped your rifle. Three, two—" He did not get to one before the outlaw tossed his rifle away and thrust his hands high above his head.

"Don't kill me. I haven't done nuthin'!"

Fargo was in no mood to bandy words with a criminal. He moved behind the kneeling man, picked up his rifle and then got the man to his feet and moved back through the dark woods to where he had run his horse into the ground.

A smile crossed Fargo's lips as he saw how efficiently his Ovaro kept the other crook at the end of a taut line. Every time the outlaw tried to get free, the horse backed, turned and even reared to pull the lariat even tighter around the man's shoulders.

"Get me free," the man bawled.

Fargo whistled, and the Ovaro settled down. The man struggled to free himself and turned to find his partner looking down the barrel of Fargo's six-gun.

"You gents have a long trip back to Fort Smith ahead of you. It's going to be even longer because you'll be walking."

Hoofbeats distracted Fargo for a split second. His heart leaped into his throat when he saw Gallegina's startled face. The Cherokee killer sawed at his horse's reins, turned and galloped away.

The two outlaws laughed and one said, "At least Buck got away. You won't be takin' him in to swing."

Fargo found himself tossed on the horns of a dilemma. He had no doubt that these two were in McGhee's gang. He could tie them up and go after Benjamin Threekiller's murderer—or just release them and go after Gallegina. Neither prospect suited him because these men were guilty as sin and should stand trial. He didn't know their names, but they rode with Mustang Jack. That put them in the company of a stone-cold killer.

But he couldn't let Gallegina ride away.

Before Fargo could gather his rope to hogtie the two, he heard more hooves pounding in his direction. Keeping the two outlaws covered, he turned to face Delacroix and Thomas.

77

"What have you rustled up here, Fargo?" drawled Thomas. "Could it be two of them boys with McGhee?"

"You know them?" asked Fargo.

"We know all of McGhee's gang. These are small fry, but you deserve the credit—and reward—for them. It must be, oh, what do you say, Thomas? Fifty dollars apiece?" Delacroix looked amused.

"Maybe not that much. These two fish are hardly worth the effort of reelin' 'em in."

"Take custody of them," Fargo said. "I spotted the man who killed Threekiller."

"Do tell," said Delacroix. "Where'd he get off to?"

Fargo swung into the saddle and found the North Star to get his bearings. For the moment, the fitful clouds had blown away in the northern sky.

"See you back at Watie's farmhouse," Fargo said, settling his horse into a rhythmic, steady gait on Gallegina's trail. Turning the two outlaws over to the deputies was the best he could do in the situation, in spite of worries that Delacroix and Thomas were less than loyal to Judge Ringo and the law.

Cowskin Prairie stretched like an endless dark rolling ocean in front of him. Fargo crested the land-waves and slipped down the gravelly troughs as he rode after Gallegina. He put his mind to the work at hand, forcing all thought of Delacroix and Thomas away. His concentration paid off by allowing him to find the most minute trail left by the running killer on terrain not easily taking imprints of horse's hooves.

Fargo had no idea how long Gallegina had been running. He might have taken part in the hurrahing of the farmhouse and be tuckered out, as the other two from McGhee's gang had been. That would make Fargo's hunt easier.

The Cherokee killer was more prudent than the white men in McGhee's gang. He did not run his horse to death in his need to escape. Instead, he doubled back, tried to lay false trails and did other tricks intended to throw any tracker off. A lesser man might have missed the subtle clues, but not Skye Fargo. Gallegina wasted time trying to throw him off and this allowed Fargo to catch up faster than if the Indian had just lit out across the prairie.

Fargo came across Gallegina trying to back his horse up over a patch of soft turf to make it appear that he had simply vanished into thin air. Drawing his Colt, Fargo approached the Cherokee as quietly as he could. He realized Gallegina was as keyed up as he was and heard the dull thud of approaching hooves.

Swinging around, Gallegina dragged out his smoke wagon and began firing wildly. The bullets cut past Fargo's head. He was more calm and collected as he returned fire. He saw Gallegina jerk and heard a Cherokee curse. Fargo had winged him but had not knocked him from horseback. Fargo fired again, and then his Colt came up empty. He rapidly switched to his Henry, but by the time he hefted it to his shoulder, Gallegina was racing the wind.

Fargo got on the Indian's trail, eating his dust and occasionally firing in his direction until he forced Gallegina to take cover. Trying to charge the man's position proved foolish. Gallegina's fire drove Fargo back to seek cover for himself and his horse.

"Give up!" Fargo shouted from cover. "I caught you once. I can do it again. You're going to stand trial for shooting Threekiller in the back!"

He hoped to distract Gallegina, but the Cherokee did not respond. Fargo poked his head out and snatched it back fast as a hail of lead ripped past him. He returned fire until his Henry's magazine came up empty. Fargo fumbled, hunting for more rounds. He went cold inside when he realized he had no more ammunition.

Slipping his Arkansas toothpick from its sheath, Fargo scuttled along until he got to a shallow gully that would take him up near Gallegina. As he worked his way along, he froze. A rattling sound he knew all too well greeted him. Fargo reared back in time to avoid a strike by the rattlesnake. He slashed out and severed the snake's head with a single cut, then sank back and took a deep breath. That had been a close call. He skirted the still twitching prairie rattler, knowing it would not truly die until sundown the next day, and continued his hunt for Gallegina.

By the time he felt he had gone far enough, a dread settled on Fargo. He popped up over the lip of the gully, ready for a hand-to-hand fight with the Cherokee.

All he saw was emptiness. Fargo scrambled up and stood where Gallegina had fired at him. Spent brass lay at his feet. He saw faint footprints leading away and knew Gallegina had retreated while he was dealing with the prairie rattler. The Cherokee might be lying in wait for him, or he might have ridden away without so much as a backward glance. Fargo had not heard the pounding of horse's hooves, but he had been distracted enough that he could have missed them.

Fargo wiped off his bloody knife on knee-high grass, sheathed his Arkansas toothpick and returned to where he had left his Henry. He hated giving up the chase for Gallegina, but fetching more ammo before going after the Indian again was more prudent. Better to waste time and be alive to catch Threekiller's murderer than to end up buzzard food out on the desolate prairie.

Swinging into the saddle, Fargo retraced his path to where he had left Delacroix and Thomas with their captives. They had gone. Their tracks headed back toward Stand Watie's farm, giving him a moment of doubt about them.

He rode steadily, occasionally taking his bearings to be sure he was not off course. When he found the road leading to the Watie farm, he knew he could get more ammunition and get on Gallegina's trail soon after dawn. Fargo went to the front of the farm and was not unduly surprised to see Stand Watie come out, rifle in his hands.

"Fargo," the Cherokee said. It was neither greeting nor warning.

"I almost caught Gallegina, but he got away when I ran out of ammo."

"We have ammo," Watie said.

"Did you catch many of the men shooting up your brother's place?" Fargo asked.

"They were white men. Possibly from the gang you seek."

"Mustang Jack McGhee and his men," Fargo said. "At least I caught two of them for you. We'll have to discuss jurisdiction since they're wanted for trial back in Fort Smith. You can telegraph Judge Ringo and—" Fargo stopped when he saw Watie's expression.

"What's wrong?" he asked.

"What are you going on about? There were no outlaws brought to me."

"Delacroix and Thomas took them into custody after I ran them down," Fargo protested. "Are they back?"

"They are," Watie said, frowning. He lifted the muzzle of his rifle and pointed across the yard to the side of the barn where two men sat. From the tiny glow Fargo knew one of the men smoked a cigarette. Fargo swung his reins around a hitching post and stormed over to where the deputies relaxed.

"Watie said there weren't any outlaws captured. What happened to the pair I caught?"

"Fargo," said Delacroix, puffing on the cigarette. He handed it to his partner. Thomas sucked in a lungful of smoke and let it out slowly.

"What happened?" Fargo demanded.

"We had a bit of the bad luck come upon us," Delacroix said. "I didn't tell old Stone Face over there because it would only cause more trouble. Watie was looking for someone to hang for shooting up his brother's place. I don't think he would take it well if he found out two of them got away from us."

"And it'd make us look like danged fools," added Thomas, finishing the cigarette. "We feel awful about bein' duped like that. Don't we, Delacroix?"

The other deputy laughed ruefully. "Reckon so. They suckered us good."

Fargo wasn't sure he wanted to hear the details because every word would be a lie. If he had any doubts about these two being in cahoots with McGhee, they were gone now.

10

"You're looking mighty spooked, Fargo," Delacroix said, eyeing him closely. "If anything, it's us who ought to be spooked after losing those two owlhoots."

"What are your plans?" Fargo asked.

"Can't say we cotton much to bein' made fools of," said Thomas. The deputy picked his teeth with a pen-knife. "Seems you got a score to settle, too. So why don't we all ride on out and get them boys back? Might even spot the Injun that killed your friend."

"That would be a feather in your cap," Delacroix went on, as if picking up his partner's thoughts. "You get Gallegina, we get the McGhee gang and take them back to Fort Smith, we all look like heroes."

Fargo knew what would happen if he rode out with these two. He would get another slug in the back. This time he could not count on them missing.

"Sounds like something I might have thought up," Fargo said. "I need to get more ammo from Watie." He led his Ovaro around to the side of the Watie farmhouse, then went to the front door and knocked. He was aware of how Delacroix and Thomas watched him the way a hungry cat watches a bird before it pounces. They were playing with him and enjoying every instant of it.

"What can I do for you?" asked Saladin Watie, coming to the door.

The young man tried to look rough and tough and almost made it. Fargo figured that within a few years Saladin would not have to try. He would make a commanding figure.

"Your pa said I could get some ammunition for my Colt and for my Henry rifle."

Saladin stepped back and let Fargo inside. The house was small and neat, well kept and odd only in that boxes of rifles lined one wall and large crates of ammunition were stacked at the rear of the living room.

"Take what you need," Saladin said, looking intently at Fargo.

After he had stuffed the needed ammo into his pockets, Fargo looked up at the boy. "Well?" he asked. "What is it you want to say?"

"Those lawmen with you. The ones who hail from Fort Smith. They are going to kill you."

Fargo laughed humorlessly. The lawmen's intentions were plain even to a sprout hardly fifteen years old.

"They'll try," Fargo said. "Don't bet on them succeeding."

"So you know?" This seemed to raise Fargo's worth in the boy's dark eyes. "They might be part of the gang you seek."

"Tell your father that," Fargo said. "I'm going to bring in the man who killed Benjamin Threekiller, then clear Seth. Unless I'm badly mistaken, either Delacroix or Thomas was the one who tried to shoot me. One of them's the one who ought to stand trial. Not Seth Threekiller."

Saladin nodded sagely but said nothing. Fargo found this more disturbing than anything else about the boy. He knew when to hold his tongue.

"You'll make a great chief one day," Fargo said, going to the window on the far side of the house away the barn. He raised the window sash and lithely slipped through. In seconds he was on his Ovaro and riding away, leaving behind the two deputies—for the time being. Fargo had no illusions about deceiving them for long.

He circled and headed for the stretch of prairie where he thought he could pick up Gallegina's tracks. So far this night he had accomplished much and had it all stolen away by the treachery of the two deputies. Fargo wanted something to show for being shot at so much and putting in so many hours staring at the grassy sod covering the prairie, hunting for the slightest hoofprint or blade of broken grass.

Fargo had been gone only a short while before the hairs on the back of his neck rose as if he rode near a raging thunderstorm. He doubled back, got to a rise and saw Delacroix and Thomas on his trail. Both rode silently with their rifles resting in the crooks of their arms. They were ready for anything, including ventilating him the instant they spotted him.

He could tangle with them, or he could try to lose them and find Gallegina. Fargo knew he had to do something about the deputies soon or they would gun him down and claim that the McGhee gang had done it. They might be in cahoots with McGhee or simply out for whatever they could find. A man like Mustang Jack McGhee might pay well to have two lawmen ride in circles for long days, then return to tell Judge Ringo they had found nothing. Or these two might have become deputies at McGhee's urging. Fargo put nothing past the wily gang leader.

Rather than take them on, he got his bearings, turned and rode steadily for the Threekiller farm. He needed help to capture the renegade lawmen.

"Oh, Skye, you're back!" cried Anna, rushing into his arms. The sun rose over his shoulder and cast golden light on the dark-haired beauty's face. She might have been an angel come to earth. He kissed her and then gently pushed her back.

"What's wrong?" she asked. "It's Seth, isn't it? Watie's got him!"

"Watie's holding him for trial," he said, "but I can get him free."

"Not from Stand Watie," Anne denied. "Father always said he was a terrible man and that John Ross's only mistake was not killing him when he had a chance."

"What do you mean?" Fargo asked in spite of his need to tell her what he wanted to.

"Why, I thought you knew. The Ketoowah Society tried to kill Watie, his brother and two others in his family years ago. They succeeded with his uncle and father but missed him and Elias."

"Ketoowah?" he asked, confused.

"A secret society that operates only at night, but everyone knows John Ross is behind them. They signal their membership to others in the society by placing crossed pins on their clothing. They tried to stop Watie and the others in his family from gaining power and failed."

"So that's why Watie is so mad at Ross," he said. For all his kindly appearance, there was more to John Ross than met the eye. He was not above murder in the dead of night to achieve his ends.

"Father said Watie should hang for all he has done. He is dividing the Cherokee Nation, and if he has Seth, why, he will surely murder him!"

"He won't," Fargo said firmly, "if I turn over the man responsible for the crime Seth is charged with. That man is after me—the men," he amended. "They're the deputies I rode into Indian Territory with."

"They aren't really lawmen?" Anna asked. It was her turn to look confused.

"They probably are legally sworn deputies, but they are also in league with McGhee. They're on my tail right now because they have to stop me or Seth will go free and the man who murdered your father will be put on trial."

"What do you want me to do, Skye?" Anna looked lovely and game for anything he wanted. He quickly explained and then went to prepare. It wouldn't be long before Delacroix and Thomas came poking around.

Fargo had barely climbed to the roof of the Threekiller house when he spotted the two men coming through the gate leading out onto the road. They had been keyed up before. Now they were a pair of raw nerves, ready to react at the slightest hint of trouble. Fargo flattened himself, partially hidden by an attic window that poked up and out from the sharply slanted roof.

"Good morning," Anna greeted the two lawmen.

Fargo heard the tension in her voice. So did Delacroix and Thomas.

"Where is the son of a bitch?" demanded Thomas.

"I beg your pardon!" Anna cried indignantly. "That's no way to speak to a lady."

"You're nothing but a whore, as far as I can see," Thomas said. "Where's Fargo?"

"If I knew, I wouldn't tell you. Your manners are terrible."

Fargo saw Delacroix incline his head in Anna's direction, giving Thomas silent instructions. Fargo started to stand on the roof and shoot the man from the saddle but he lost his chance. Thomas dropped to the ground out of sight. As long as Thomas was hidden from view, he could harm Anna. Fargo cursed under his breath. She had not gone along with the men the way he had told her. He wanted them to come around the side of the house hunting for him. A simple drop from the roof onto the deputies would have knocked them both to the ground as they rode under him. Anna had a shotgun ready to come and cover them, if he needed help.

Now all that planning was for naught.

Fargo heard Anna scream and then the door banged as Thomas dragged her into the house.

He could wait no longer. Fargo ran four quick paces and then launched himself through the air. Delacroix saw him at the last instant. The Cajun's eyes opened and he tried to swing his rifle around. Then Fargo's shoulder crushed into his chest, knocking him from his horse. Fargo landed on top of the deputy. He had his fists clenched to slug him but it wasn't necessary. The fall had knocked Delacroix out.

Fargo ripped away the man's rifle and tossed his six-shooter under the front porch. From inside came Anna's screams. Fargo whipped out his Colt and rushed to the door, only to narrowly miss getting his head blown off by a shotgun blast.

"Damn you, Fargo," came Thomas's taunting voice. "Why won't you die? Delacroix missed you when you found McGhee's camp. Now I plumb missed you with a scattergun the li'l lady had waitin' for me."

"Are you all right, Anna?" Fargo called.

"Oh, she's fine as frog's fur," came Thomas's mocking words. "I'm gonna find out how fine after I kill you."

Fargo knew Thomas baited him so he would make a mistake. Fargo kicked open the door and ducked back immediately. The second barrel discharged, ripping through wood. The time was now or never. If Fargo let Thomas think on it, Anna's life would be forfeit. He would try using her has a hostage, a shield, a way of getting his revenge.

Fargo dived through the door and hit the floor hard, his six-gun blazing. The slugs tore past Thomas and drove him into the rear bedroom. Anna jerked free, ducked and got away. Fargo frantically motioned for her to get to one side of the room. She was in shock, and it took a few precious seconds for her to understand. Only when she had taken refuge behind the sofa did he go after Thomas.

Bursting into the bedroom, six-shooter ready for action, Fargo found himself all alone. Thomas had never hesitated once he lost Anna as a hostage. He had gone out the bedroom window.

"Stay down," Fargo said, retracing his path to the front porch. He got off a couple shots at Thomas's retreating back but missed. The range was too great. Fargo twisted around and trained his pistol on the still unconscious Delacroix.

"Don't, Skye. Don't kill him like that," Anna said, her hand on his gun arm.

"I'm not going to plug him, no matter how much he deserves it. He's my proof that your brother is innocent. Stand Watie will listen to his confession. I'll see to that," he said grimly.

Anna looked skeptical. "What of the other one?" She pointed in the direction Thomas had ridden.

"He'll keep riding until he reaches California or joins up with McGhee," Fargo guessed. He hesitated because he could not be sure Thomas would do either. If the renegade deputy returned, Anna would be alone and helpless.

"I'll reload the shotgun," she said, as if she had read his mind. "Get that one to Watie and free Seth."

Fargo heard the unspoken "if you can" in her declaration. This made him all the more determined to free Seth and see to it that Delacroix was brought to justice, even if it was Cherokee justice.

"I don't need to hear more," Stand Watie said, glaring at Delacroix. "You have done nothing but sow discord among us. You have not even limited it to the Cherokee Nation, but have also engaged the Chickasaw, Choctaw, Creek, and Seminole in your vile schemes and lawlessness."

"I've done nothing to harm your people," Delacroix said, summoning some backbone. He straightened and glared at Fargo and Seth Threekiller. "They are the ones stirring the pot. They are the ones who support John Ross in his war against you."

"I have your confession that, while you did not try to shoot Mr. Fargo in the back, your partner did. This clears Seth Threekiller of the charges against him."

"I'm free?" asked Seth, eyes wide with amazement. He could not believe Stand Watie let him go this easily.

"You are. There is no need for a trial in light of the confession," He fixed his cold eyes on Delacroix. Watie went on. "Shackle this one and put him to work in the fields with the rest of the slaves."

"What?" Fargo stepped forward. "You can't do that!"

"He is guilty. His partner fired the actual shots at you and will be tried for attempted murder when he is caught. My men will scour the country until they find him."

"You can't enslave him. That's wrong."

"He must pay for his crimes against the Cherokee Nation," Watie said.

"Please," Seth said, clinging to Fargo's arm. "I . . . I don't think I can stand too much more. Get me home. Please." The plaintive note made Fargo take his first hard look at the young man. He was wan, drawn and his hands shook. He had been through hell and had never fully recovered from his earlier injury.

Fargo left Watie and the protesting Delacroix, sick to his stomach. Delacroix deserved punishment, but not being chained and put to work in the fields alongside slaves. But he could do nothing about it now. He had to see Seth home safely before dealing with Thomas, McGhee—and Delacroix.

"He's sleeping," Anna said, coming from the bedroom where Thomas had been so recently.

"Seth looked as if he were closer to passing out than sleeping," Fargo said. He saw Anna nod. Her worried expression told him her brother was in a bad way. "Why was he out on Cowskin Prairie?"

"He thought Watie had something to do with Father's death. He wasn't content with the notion that Gallegina alone was responsible."

"Seth went after the wrong man. Gallegina rides with McGhee and his gang. Watie wants him stopped as much as I—we—do."

"I couldn't get Seth to rest up and regain his strength. He is such a hothead at times." Tears welled in her eyes as she added, "Just like Father."

"Seth has your father's gift of gab. He will be diplomatic when he needs to be," Fargo said to assure her all would be fine. This quieted Anna a little. She came to him and hugged him close and buried her face in his chest.

"You've done so much for me and my family, Skye. I want to thank you."

"Is that what you call it?" he joked, seeing the look in her eyes. The hurt and confusion had vanished, replaced with growing lust.

She half turned and pressed her hip into his groin. Then Anna began rubbing like a cat against him until his growing manhood became painful. The lovely woman seemed to take some pleasure in his discomfort.

"The barn?" she asked.

"Again?" he shook his head. "It's getting mighty hot already and that stock tank out back looks inviting."

"If you're so hot, why not take off some of this hardware?" Anna's clever fingers worked on his gun belt and shirt and tugged at the buttons of his fly. By the time they reached the stock tank both were naked to the waist. Fargo figured he enjoyed the sight of Anna's gently bouncing breasts more than she liked the sight of her hairy chest.

Or maybe not. She burrowed her face in the hairy mat and licked and kissed until she was panting with need. Then it was his turn to give her the same treatment. He had liked the feel of his lips and tongue moving on her bare flesh, but he enjoyed sucking in the lust-hardened nub atop one breast much more. Fargo suckled on it until Anna moaned low with pleasure.

She clutched at his head, holding it in place. He licked up one coppery slope, toyed with the nipple, and then made his way back to the other one. He felt her legs going weak, so he scooped her up in his arms.

"It's getting *real* hot," he said.

"The weather?" she asked, a wicked grin dancing on her lips.

"Nope." Fargo heaved the woman into the water. Anna let out a squeal of glee as she hit the water. She splashed around and then surfaced. Fargo watched as she rose from the tank, her breasts now damp and even more appealing.

He wasted no time kicking off his boots and pulling free of his buckskin pants. He heaved a sigh of relief as his thick stalk was finally free of the imprisoning cloth. Standing on the edge of the stock tank, Fargo took his measure and then jumped in with a big splash.

Somehow, while he was still underwater, Anna found him. Their bodies slid along each other, touching in all the right places. For an exciting second, he felt her lips brushing over the thick knob at the end of his stalk. Then the light touch vanished, replaced with Anna's fingers stroking over his back.

He sputtered and came to the surface. The woman

reached around behind him and grabbed his buttocks. With a powerful tug, she pulled him close. His throbbing length rubbed against the wet, tangled bush between her thighs—and then Anna scissored her legs a couple times, letting the water buoy her. She spread her legs, splashed closer and jerked hard.

Fargo's entire length vanished into her clinging interior. He thought the water was going to boil with the heat blazing in both their loins.

He arched his back and shoved his hips down into hers. He felt himself sink another inch into her channel. They hung in the water, connected at the groin for several seconds. Fargo relished the heat and intimacy. Then he felt her inner muscles begin to twitch and grip down on him.

He rolled over in the water. Anna went with him, clinging tightly. They kept rolling and came back to the surface, sputtering and sloshing. Fargo reached out and pulled her in more securely. Try as he might to keep still, he began moving in and out of her clutching recess.

"Oh, Skye," Anna moaned. "You're so big. Don't hold back. I want you so!"

His hands slid down her water-slickened back and cupped her rump. He kneaded the firm flesh and used the grip to guide her hips back and forth to match his thrusts. At first he wasn't able to coordinate well. The water took away their weight but it also made it difficult for him to get any traction. Then Fargo got the hang of it and began stroking with more rhythmic movements until Anna sobbed and moaned in delight.

Fargo swallowed hard, fighting to keep from spending like a young buck with his first woman. But it was difficult to hold back. Anna was so beautiful and willing. The way her inner muscles massaged his length every time he slipped fully into her set him on fire.

The fire exploded and raged throughout his belly. He grunted as he spewed forth his load just as Anna cried out in release. They let themselves ride the waves tossing them high and then slowly floated away from each other.

Fargo paddled around watching as Anna languidly

floated on her back. Her breasts poked up delightfully and he caught occasional glimpses of the dark bush where he had just gone hunting.

"Tell me when you're ready again, Skye," she said softly.

"Ready? Again? No time soon! You plumb tuckered me out!" he exclaimed.

She swam to him, then vanished underwater. Again came the feathery touch of her lips on his organ. Fargo found himself responding and ready faster than he would have thought. After a second bout of lovemaking, they pulled themselves out of the water to dry off and rest. The only thing they had to worry about then was getting sunburned in places usually not exposed to the bright summer sun.

11

"We have enough weapons now to start our own war," Anna Threekiller observed. Scattered on the kitchen table were the rifles and shotguns her father had owned. Alongside them now rested the six-shooter and rifle Fargo had taken from Delacroix. He remembered how Stand Watie's house had been an armory and ammo dump as he shook his head. It seemed that all the Cherokees were preparing for a massacre.

"This might not be enough," he said.

Anna nodded sagely and said. "There is a war coming. I feel it in my bones, too. But this is *our* farm, and I am not going to leave."

"You have to fight for what you believe in," Fargo said. "And for what's rightly yours. In spite of your brother's faith in John Ross, he seems a mighty weak horse to hitch your wagon to."

"Watie is a killer!" flared Anna.

"He might not be much better, but he is a stronger leader."

"You said we have to fight for what we believe in," Anna said earnestly. "We have to fight against Watie and the other slaveholders. Slavery is tearing apart the Cherokee Nation."

Fargo said nothing. She was right. If she had traveled up and down the Mississippi as much as he had recently, she would have seen that slavery was doing more than breaking up the Cherokee Nation. It was also destroying the unity of the United States.

That was a bigger concern for Fargo, but he was one man against half a nation. What he could do was catch

Coot Marlowe's killer. And Ben Threekiller's. If he could restore some semblance of law and order to Judge Ringo's district it would go a ways toward smoothing ruffled feathers on all sides in Indian Territory.

More than this, it was something he could do right away. He had the feeling of sitting on a powder keg watching the fuse burn toward him. Action had to be taken soon or everything west of the Mississippi would explode.

"It's horrible how the outlaws come here to hide out. And nobody tries to chase them out," Anna said.

"Watie has a vigilante posse patrolling Cowskin Prairie," he told her. "I don't know how successful it is because all the men have farms of their own to tend."

"Ross has recruited John Drew to assemble a militia to enforce the laws of the tribe, but Drew is a fool," Anna said harshly.

"Will you be all right if I leave?" he asked.

"Seth is . . . healing," she said unconvincingly.

This worried Fargo as much as tracking down the killers. Seth Threekiller had slipped into a coma on his return to the farm. He thrashed about in his bed, shouting curses and grabbing for ghosts that were not there—except in his troubled mind. Whether he had picked up a fever or simply retreated into himself because of all that had happened to him was something beyond Fargo's experience. He had seen men will themselves to die, but this was different.

"Maybe you should get him into Tahlequah to see a doctor," he said.

"I won't leave the farm."

The firmness in the woman's jaw convinced Fargo she would defend her home to her last breath.

"Do you want me to go to town and send out the doctor?"

"No, Seth will be fine," she said, looking out the window in the direction of their fields. "He would never miss harvest."

Fargo did not point out to her the backbreaking work necessary before fall harvest, which was still months off.

He felt tossed on the horns of a new dilemma. Take time getting a doctor out to see Seth or ride straight away after Thomas. Either was worthwhile, but he could not do both.

Fargo felt the renegade deputy would lead him to McGhee and the rest of his gang, if he got on the trail quickly enough. There had been no evidence that the two outlaws he had captured had put up any fight to get away from Delacroix and Thomas earlier. That meant the lawmen probably knew where the gang camped. If Thomas wanted help getting his partner free of Watie's stern justice, he would recruit Mustang Jack McGhee.

"You can care for Seth by yourself? Is there a neighbor who can help?"

"Go, Skye, go after the deputy." Anna clung to him and he felt hot tears against his skin. She pushed back, turned so he could not see how she cried and shook out his buckskin shirt. "Here, you'll need this. And your own six-gun." She handed them to him, her eyes averted.

He lifted her chin, stared into her dark, fathomless eyes and then kissed her. Fargo knew she was strong and determined and would prevail. He left quickly before he changed his mind. His duty to Judge Ringo—and Coot Marlowe's memory—was stronger than the need to fetch a doctor for Seth. The young man might need nothing but time to heal himself.

"Let's get on the trail," Fargo said to his Ovaro. The powerful stallion snorted and tossed its head, ready to once more be on the wide, open prairie.

Fargo judged the direction of Thomas's retreat and went that way. It had been almost two days since the renegade deputy had hightailed it, but Fargo found sections of the man's trail with little effort. Fargo made better time than he thought because Thomas had made no effort to hide his tracks.

By midafternoon Fargo came to the end of the trail. Thomas had led him to a meandering creek where Mustang Jack McGhee's gang camped. This presented Fargo with a real problem. As he spied on the outlaws, he saw not only McGhee but Gallegina, along with Thomas and

Ned Sondergard. The two road agents he had captured and whom the deputies had released were also in the camp talking with another pair of outlaws.

He was one man against eight. Riding in and demanding their surrender would gain him a few pounds of lead in his belly. Trying to pick them off one by one seemed unlikely to work, also.

He stroked his chin as he studied the layout of the camp. If Lady Luck rode with him, he might sneak into the camp and take out two or even three of the outlaws before the others noticed. That left him with a fight on his hands—a fight against at least five armed and murderous deperados—that he was not likely to win.

Still, he had no choice. He had to do something fast or the gang would drift on and create further havoc both here in the Cherokee Nation and across the river in Arkansas.

Fargo left his rifle in its saddle sheath and decided to take only his six-shooter and knife. Any gunfight would end in his death; he intended to get away with at least one of his targets: McGhee or Gallegina. If he nabbed Mustang Jack McGhee the rest of the gang might dance around like chickens with their heads cut off. That gave a little advantage to any lawmen on their trail. Fargo might drop off Mustang Jack and then return and catch a few more.

And Gallegina. He had to be certain to turn over the Cherokee killer to John Ross—or Stand Watie. He had yet to decide which man afforded the best avenue for a fair trial. Fargo knew Gallegina was guilty, but wouldn't condone a necktie party. If Gallegina swung, and Fargo thought he should, it had to happen after a jury trial.

The gathering twilight was disturbed by occasional fireflies winking on and off. Fargo slipped like a shadow down the hillside, his occasional small sound covered by the burbling of the creek as it ran across the prairie. He circled and came up behind the spot where McGhee had stretched his bedroll. The man spoke with Thomas and two others. Using a stick McGhee drew a map in the dry dirt and spoke too low for Fargo to overhear. Whatever the outlaw leader plotted, it was bound to cause woe for someone.

Fargo settled down behind a fallen log and endured the termites working on the wood inches from his nose as he waited for his chance to grab McGhee. If Thomas had not been so intent on arguing every point, the planning would have gone faster. But Fargo was a patient man. He would not rush this capture.

Thomas finally walked off, leaving McGhee with Sondergard and another of his gang. They continued to plot and plan until a sentry at the far side of their camp hooted like an owl. Fargo blinked at the speed with which McGhee rubbed out the dusty map and grabbed for his rifle and tack.

Fargo hardly knew what was going on as McGhee and his men abandoned most of their belongings in favor of saddling their horses. Whatever the signal had meant, it startled McGhee and his men into swift retreat.

Fargo saw his chance to take McGhee prisoner vanishing before his eyes. He got his feet under him and rose, ready to run after the outlaw chief.

Bullets ripped through the camp as he exposed himself, but none came from the outlaws. They were already galloping away into the dusk. Fargo threw himself flat and began wiggling like a sidewinder to get out of the camp. He had no idea who was hurrahing the outlaw campsite, but they were not aiming. Every shot went wild.

Even as he thought that the gunfire was random, a bullet sang hot and deadly past his cheek. Fargo jerked and touched the wound. It bled freely but did not seem serious. He changed direction and crawled back upslope to where he had left his Ovaro.

"There's one of them devil. Git 'im boys!" went up the cry.

It took Fargo only an instant to realize he had been seen, and the men attacking McGhee's camp were now after him. He swung into the saddle, ready to ride like the wind. He had no idea who was after McGhee, but he knew they were not inclined to sit and chew the fat until they determined he was not one of the gang.

Head low, he got his horse into a gallop. The darkness masked him quickly, but the prairie turned dangerous with gopher holes and ravines that suddenly appeared. Fargo reined back, and cut sharply away from the course he had ridden, hoping to circle and get away from the men pursuing him so aggressively. It took only a few seconds for him to realize he had not put enough distance between himself and his pursuers for this trick to work. They also changed their route about where he had and clung to him like flypaper.

Fargo changed direction again, this time heading back toward McGhee's camp. The men might not think he would ride into the main body of their posse, if they were a posse.

"He's goin' back to his camp. Back, men, git on back!"

The instant Fargo heard this command, he changed direction again but still could not make enough speed on the uneven terrain to put much distance between himself and his pursuers. Yet another time, Fargo changed his tactics. He rode through a stand of trees, hunting for the right limb.

As he rode under an oak, he stood upright in the stirrups, grabbed and swung free of his Ovaro. The horse kept running. He hated to use it to decoy away the riders, but he had no choice until he found out who was after him and how many there were.

"I hear 'im. He's still goin' like a bat outta hell!" cried the leader of the band. They pounded under the tree where Fargo crouched on the limb, looking down at them. The night hid their identities. If Stand Watie had sent the men, he might have surrendered and taken his chances with the slaveholder. Fargo couldn't abide the man's ways, but Watie was an honorable enough man otherwise, and talking his way out of trouble was possible.

Not knowing who chased him complicated his situation. McGhee and his gang were getting away—and Fargo had to escape this posse. He waited until what he thought was the last man in the band passed beneath the limb where he squatted. Catching his breath, then releasing it in a gust, Fargo launched himself.

He crashed into the rider and knocked him from his horse. The man landed flat on his back so hard the air gushed from his lungs. Gasping weakly, the fallen rider tried to move, to turn, to breathe. Fargo wasted no time running after the frightened horse and grabbing its reins. He pulled it around without trying to soothe it. There was no time. With a hop, he mounted and turned around—to find himself staring down the barrel of a six-shooter.

12

"Whoa, don't go getting an itchy trigger finger," Fargo said, his hands rising to grab a handful of diamond-hard stars in the sky above. He considered his chances of getting away and quickly saw he would end up in a shallow grave if he tried.

"You're under arrest," the man said, the six-gun unwavering on Fargo's midriff.

"I was after McGhee and his gang. You upset the applecart because I was ready to nab him."

"McGhee?"

"Mustang Jack McGhee is the leader of the gang and is wanted in Fort Smith for murder." Fargo's words tasted of bile on his tongue. He had wasted so much time in Indian Territory hunting men for other crimes. Coot Marlowe had gone unavenged long enough.

"White eyes are always wanted somewhere. They would not come to the Cherokee Nation unless they were running from something. None of you ever runs *to* our land." The Indian's words were as bitter as Fargo's, but for other reasons.

"I'd be pleased as punch to let you be if I could take McGhee back to Fort Smith. And I have another one of his gang—or one who's riding with the gang—that I need to bring in for trial."

"That's a mighty curious way of saying what you mean," the man said.

Fargo took the Indian's desire to talk it out as a good thing. He wanted to hear what Fargo said rather than simply silencing him and taking him in for some magistrate to try.

"Gallegina is the killer's name. He wants to be called Buck, but he's a backshooter by any name. He killed Benjamin Threekiller."

"Gallegina's one of Watie's men," came the sharp response. The man moved closer but his face remained hidden in the shadow of his broad-brimmed hat. Fargo saw he was dressed in traditional Cherokee fashion except for the curious crossed pins fastened on the front of his red cloth shirt.

"Pins," Fargo said, remembering what Anna had said. Those pins marked members of a secret society backing John Ross against Stand Watie, following their principal chief's clandestine orders. "You're a member of the Ketoowah Society."

"You know of us? You? A white man?"

"I hear of many important men," Fargo said. "All speak of your heroism. But the outlaws are getting away. I want them caught and tried as much as you. We can chatter all night, or we can get on their trail. McGhee and the others lit out only a few minutes ago."

"They were more vigilant than I thought," the Cherokee said. "They ran at first warning. But we caught you. We have one of the outlaws."

"You work for John Ross, don't you?" Everything pointed to it. The crossed pins, the contempt with which Stand Watie was mentioned, the way the man had perked up when Gallegina's name came into the dialogue—it all told Fargo this posse had been sent out to counter Watie's roving militia.

"What do you care?"

"Are you John Drew?" This was another name Fargo had heard.

"I ride with him." The shot in the dark had hit its mark. "I am Daniel Pathkiller." Pathkiller tipped his head slightly as he studied Fargo. "I do not know you. I have never seen you before, yet you know much. How is this possible?"

"Tracking down McGhee—and Gallegina—has taken me into strange places while I've been in Indian Territory." Fargo didn't want to say he had learned more about Cherokee politics and the various groups fighting for control than he wanted to know.

"You know Chief Ross?"

"I've met him a couple times. I was displeased that he let Gallegina escape after I turned him over for trial."

"You are Fargo?"

Fargo's eyebrows arched. "I am."

"Chief Ross spoke of you as an ally." Pathkiller lowered his six-shooter. Fargo relaxed a little for the first time, but remained wary. The tide could turn against him fast.

"Our desires are the same, wanting Gallegina tried for Threekiller's murder," Fargo said carefully.

"If Gallegina rides with the white-eyes outlaws, then they are our enemies, too," declared Pathkiller.

"How good are your men at tracking?" asked Fargo, anxious to get in the saddle after McGhee again.

"The Light Horse Brigade is the best among the Five Civilized Tribes!" Pathkiller bragged.

"Light Horse troopers," mused Fargo. He held his opinion of calling this ragtag band with such a fine military cognomen. If they could ride and fight, he didn't care if they were the least bit military.

"They went northwest," Pathkiller said, glancing at a man who had ridden up. Fargo did not see how either man signaled the other, but they understood. That was good enough for him.

"Let's ride," Fargo said. He turned to fetch his Ovaro. As he made his way into the darkness, he felt the Indians' gaze on his back. He waited for a bullet or an arrow to end his life, but death did not come. When he rode back to join Pathkiller, he was greeted like a member of the Light Horse Brigade.

The sun hammered Fargo and beat him down. He sweated heavily and wanted to take off his buckskin shirt, but refused to waste the time that would require. The Cherokees were good trackers and had stayed on McGhee's trail as diligently as he could. The only trouble was the outlaw's determination to leave them far behind.

Once McGhee had taken out of his camp, he had never slackened his pace or even stopped more than a few minutes to let his gang water and rest their horses.

But as they slowly narrowed the distance Fargo now felt it in his bones that the outlaws were within his grasp.

"Not far," Pathkiller said suddenly. The Cherokee sniffed the air like a hunting wolf. Fargo had detected nothing as they rode across Cowskin Prairie. He figured Pathkiller was only showing off and had received some silent signal from the scouts ahead on the trail.

"How are we going to take them?" Fargo asked. "Try to surround them or simply ride through the middle of their camp and scatter them so we can pick them off one by one later?"

Pathkiller looked at him sharply. "How did you know they have camped?"

Fargo kept from grinning. He had not known until that moment.

"I've lived on the frontier all my life," he said, "and I know many things. Do we charge their camp and send them running again? Their horses are exhausted and cannot go too far. Or do we try to get them to surrender without fighting?"

"We circle and force them to surrender." Pathkiller said, eyeing Fargo suspiciously. He still wondered how Fargo had guessed so accurately where the outlaws were. The Cherokee had no idea Fargo was as careful an observer of men as he was of trail spoor.

Fargo checked his Colt, made sure his Henry carried a full magazine, then nodded.

They rode slowly to the end of a narrow valley. Less than a hundred yards ahead of them sat two scouts, the ones who had already sent the information about McGhee's gang to Pathkiller. They lifted their rifles and made waving motions, then pointed toward a narrow stream meandering down the middle of the valley. Without a word, Pathkiller and his Light Horse troopers headed for the stream. Fargo followed, knowing the scouts had found the best route to the outlaws' camp.

Single file, they rode up the stream. The horses' hooves

made soft splashing sounds that were hidden by the normal bubbling, rushing sound of the creek over stones. Along the stream grew tall trees, some willows but more elm and post oak that hid their approach. After fifteen minutes of riding, the scouts sent the signal back down the line until it reached Fargo.

Half continued upstream, then cut to their right to block retreat. Pathkiller and the remainder of his troopers waited a few more minutes, then rode away from the stream.

Fargo was a latecomer to the fight that started, more because he was at the end of the line rather than any intent on wanting to avoid conflict. Again McGhee's sentries had spotted the approaching troopers quickly. Unable to run further because of their tired horses, the outlaws opened up with a deadly fusillade that left one of Pathkiller's men dead and two more wounded.

Fargo whipped out his Colt and fired at one outlaw trying to get a bead on Pathkiller. His bullet caught the gunman's forearm. The outlaw screeched in agony and spun around, clutching his wounded arm. Fargo shot forward, kicked and caught the man in the back of the head with the toe of his boot. The man dropped to his hands and knees, stunned.

"Thank you," called Pathkiller, already turning his attention elsewhere.

The Light Horse troopers engaged in a hard fight with the outlaws. Trapped rats came to Fargo's mind. The trap sprung by Pathkiller ought to have been stronger and backed by more planning, but he understood the man's need to capture McGhee's gang as fast as he could. McGhee was as slippery as an eel.

Fargo ducked when an outlaw—one he had captured and who had been let go by Delacroix and Thomas—swung a tree limb at him. The wood smashed into Fargo's shoulder, jarring him. The outlaw attacked from the left side, forcing Fargo to reach in front of himself to get a shot off. When he did, the bullet went wide.

"Give up," Fargo ordered. "We've got you surrounded."

"You'll never take us. You'll never get Mustang Jack!" cried the outlaw.

Fargo launched himself from the Ovaro and tackled the outlaw, knocking him to the ground. Somehow, he had dived under a tornado of lead that sang back and forth across the campsite. When the thunderous roar of discharging guns died down, Fargo looked up and saw many of the troopers clutching wounds.

Then he was upset and clubbed to one side by the outlaw he had knocked down. Flat on his back, Fargo cocked his Colt and pointed it at the outlaw. The man seemed to be hung by a thread, unsure whether to run or attack.

"How much lead can you carry in your belly before you fall over?" Fargo asked.

The outlaw reluctantly put up his hands. Fargo got to his feet and saw Pathkillers men were milling around in confusion.

"I've got one. How about you?" Fargo called to the leader of the Light Horse troopers.

"We have one, also," Pathkiller said, herding another of McGhee's men to where Fargo had the drop on his captive.

"That's all? Where's McGhee?" he demanded. Pathkiller shrugged.

Fargo looked around and saw that most of the gang had escaped. At no time during the assault had he seen McGhee, but as he looked around his sharp eyes caught sight of thick green leaves rustling strangely in a tall oak tree.

"Take him," Fargo said to Pathkiller. He made sure the posse leader understood he was swinging his six-shooter off target and toward the tree limb.

Fargo strode forward until he had a good angle to see up through the canopy of leaves. He cocked his six-shooter and fired. The slug ripped through the leaves and produced a loud yelp of surprise.

"Come on down," Fargo called. He moved to a spot where he had a better view through a bare spot and saw

Gallegina scuttling down the tree trunk like an overgrown squirrel.

"I'll trade for McGhee," Gallegina shouted. "Let me go, I tell you where McGhee is!"

"Come on down and we'll talk," Fargo said. He had no intention of trading Benjamin Threekiller's murderer for Coot Marlowe's. He wanted both to answer for their crimes.

A ruckus behind Fargo caused him to spin around and go into a crouch, his six-shooter thrust in front of him. The man he had caught and turned over to Pathkiller was making a bid for freedom, wrestling with the Cherokee. The other Light Horse troopers either did not notice or simply stared dully.

"Stop it!" Fargo barked. The outlaw swung Pathkiller around as a shield. Fargo aimed and fired. His bullet went between Pathkiller's arm and chest and winged the outlaw. As the man stumbled back grabbing for the bloody wound in his side, Pathkiller acted. He slammed his elbow back and caught the outlaw in the side of the head. This drove the man to the ground.

"Don't," Fargo said, whirling around to cover the second outlaw Pathkiller had captured. The man's hands went up slowly, but his eyes darted around as he hunted for a way to escape.

"Get over here," bellowed Fargo to the other Cherokees. "Get your guns out and cover these men until you get them hog-tied!"

The troopers responded sluggishly, but they came to their leader's aid. Fargo turned back to Gallegina. He let out a low curse when he saw what the man had done. Rather than drop to the ground, Gallegina had jumped from the limb of the oak to the next tree. He might have kept jumping because he was nowhere to be seen.

Fargo cursed a blue streak as he stalked along under the arboreal highway, looking up at the broken twigs and trying to find where the leaves had freshly fallen to the ground due to Gallegina's frantic retreat. The path wasn't hard to follow, especially when he found where the murderous Cherokee had jumped to the ground and run off, but he had grown careless letting the murderer get away so easily. If Gallegina had taken it into his head, he could have plugged Fargo in the back, as he had Threekiller.

From the distance between the footprints, Fargo figured Gallegina was running hellbent for leather. He picked up his pace, knowing the man was going to exhaust himself quickly. His fear would drain his stamina, too, and Fargo counted on finding him before much longer.

Gallegina had reached the side of the valley and was working his way up it, pawing and digging at the hill in his haste to reach the top and vanish over it.

Fargo cocked his pistol and took careful aim. His finger drew back on the trigger. His Colt bucked and a plume of dirt jumped up in front of Gallegina. The startled Cherokee yelped, scrambled wildly, lost his footing and slid kicking and clawing down the hillside, coming to rest at Fargo's feet. Fargo pointed his six-gun directly between the frightened man's eyes.

"You want to come along now?"

"You no kill me?"

"Don't tempt me," Fargo said.

"No shoot, I give up!" Gallegina had gone from the arrogant backshooting murderer to a sniveling toad. For two cents Fargo would have plugged him. It was a good thing there was no one there to make the offer.

Fargo got Gallegina stumbling back in the direction of Pathkiller and his mostly useless Light Horse Brigade, intent that he would see Gallegina back to Tahlequah personally.

13

Fargo rode into Tahlequah, again with Benjamin Three-killer's killer in tow. He had a rope around Gallegina's middle and the Cherokee's hands secured behind his back. If Gallegina made the slightest move to escape, all Fargo had to do was tug on the line and unseat him. He had promised Gallegina he would drag him the rest of the way to the Tahlequah jailhouse if this happened anywhere along the road to the Cherokee capital. The threat had worked well because Gallegina had ridden along sullenly, not saying a single word.

Looking around, Fargo saw how Pathkiller and his Light Horse Brigade surrounded the other outlaws they had caught—two of the McGhee gang. One of them Fargo had already caught—one who had been released by Delacroix and Thomas. How Fargo wished they had caught Thomas and Mustang Jack McGhee instead!

As before, he had been faced with the dilemma of bringing in a known killer and letting the rest of the road agents escape or trusting to fate that Gallegina got to jail with Pathkiller's posse. No matter how he tried, Fargo could not call the Light Horse Brigade a militia. Pathkiller and the others lacked even rudimentary military order and training and had been formed on the spur of the moment to counter Stand Watie's men patrolling up north on Cowskin Prairie.

Cheers went up as Pathkiller rode along, greeting people in the street by name. He was more intent on basking in the sudden fame the foray against the outlaws brought than he was in locking up his prisoners. This disgusted

Fargo. Trouble brewed in the Cherokee Nation and too many men sought only personal fame and fortune.

That was the Cherokee leader's problem, he decided. Let John Ross deal with it and his relations with it and his relations with the other four tribes surrounding the Cherokee Nation.

"Get down," Fargo said.

Gallegina glared at him. The Indian lifted his dark eyes and fixed them on the courthouse barely twenty yards distant. Fargo saw the muscles tensing in his jaw as Gallegina prepared to make a bid for freedom. Circumventing the attempt was simple. Fargo tugged hard on the rope around the man's middle, unbalancing him.

"Aieee!" Gallegina cried as he toppled from the saddle. Fargo had considered letting the man crash to the ground, but he wanted to deliver his prisoner in good condition. A quick stride forward let Fargo catch the falling man and break his fall enough so that though Gallegina's knees banged the ground, he was otherwise undamaged.

"Walk," Fargo said. He glanced over his shoulder where Pathkiller and his troopers still greeted the townspeople. Anyone coming into town right now would think Pathkiller had won a war rather than merely captured two outlaws while letting the most dangerous members of the gang escape.

He hoped the troopers wouldn't get so caught up in the public adulation that they let their two prisoners escape.

"You can never prove anything. Chief Ross let me go before. Why do you think he won't do it again?"

"Let you go?" Fargo laughed harshly. "That's not the way I heard it. You made some kind of a deal with McGhee, and he sprung you. You've got a jail escape added to your list of crimes." Fargo kept tugging until he got Gallegina up the steps. The man's attitude changed radically.

"Please, don't turn me over to Chief Ross!" Gallegina pleaded. "He will hang me! He thinks I ride for Stand Watie!"

"You shot Benjamin Threekiller in the back. Do you deserve any less than a hemp necktie?"

"You don't understand. Threekiller supported Ross. Watie told me to kill him. It's Watie who should be on trial! Let him hang!"

Fargo reckoned Stand Watie had a lot to answer for, but he had seen nothing to indicate Watie had told Gallegina to kill anyone. For all that, he saw nothing tying Gallegina to Watie in any way. Mustang Jack McGhee had come to the man's rescue before, and Ross had been too weak to hold onto him. That was a black mark against Ross, but Fargo had to deal with it.

"Come on." He dragged a reluctant Gallegina into the foyer, whipped the rope around the balustrade of the stairs leading to the second floor and went to the heavy wood door leading into Ross's office. Fargo rapped sharply, then went in.

John Ross looked up, startled. His thinning hair was in wild disarray and from the wrinkles in his clothing it was obvious he had slept in them. Fargo saw evidence that the principal chief had spent the night on a nearby sofa. With him was a ramrod straight man, thin to the point of emaciation, who stared daggers at Fargo for interrupting their no doubt important conference.

"Mr. Fargo, how nice to see you again," Ross said with no conviction. "Have you met Colonel Drew?"

"You and the one responsible for the Light Horse Brigade?" Fargo asked. He shook his head in disgust. John Drew was no more a military man than Pathkiller, who was still outside enjoying the adulation of the crowd.

"I am, sir. Chief Ross knows you. I do not."

Fargo ignored the colonel and spoke directly to John Ross. "I've brought Gallegina in again. Can you hold him this time?"

"The raid that freed him left one jailer dead, Mr. Fargo. I assure you we did not let him go lightly."

"Might be that you need more jailers," Fargo said, "since Pathkiller's got two of McGhee's gang. From everything I've learned of Mustang Jack, he's not an hombre who lets his men rot in jail. He's inclined to rescue them or kill them trying to get them free. That way there's no one to spill his plans."

"Your knowledge of the lawless element is appreciated," Drew said caustically. "If you will excuse us, we have important matters under discussion."

"More important than bringing in a man who gunned down one of your staunchest supporters?" Again Fargo ignored John Drew and directed his words toward the Cherokee chief. "Benjamin Threekiller went to his death supporting you. How's it going to look to your other backers if you let Gallegina off scot-free?"

"He will not be *allowed* to go, uh, 'scot-free' as you call it, Mr. Fargo." John Ross heaved a deep sigh that rattled the old man's bones. "A death here and there matters less than dealing with the threat posed by Stand Watie. His army threatens to split our nation down the middle."

"Mind the big items and to hell with the little ones—like justice for a murdered man?"

"Mr. Fargo, please," Ross said. "I know you are emotionally involved with this, but—"

"Get Gallegina into a cell. I have McGhee and the rest of his gang to catch," Fargo said. He stormed from Ross's office, angrier than he should have been. The Cherokee Nation owed him nothing, and he owed the people nothing, but he saw bringing Gallegina to trial as simple justice for Anna and Seth. Let Ross look at the civil war brewing in his nation all he wanted, but Fargo intended to be certain Gallegina was tried for his crime.

That was only fair.

Fargo had to hand it to John Ross. The principal chief wasted no time bringing Gallegina to trial. Fargo had worried he would be stuck in Tahlequah for weeks or even months while the Cherokee chief fiddled around finding a judge, attorneys, prosecutors and witnesses. Instead, Ross sat judge. Two Cherokees Fargo had not seen before worked both for and against Gallegina. From the opening statements, Fargo approved of the prosecutor. He spoke well and won over the jury of a dozen men early with his depiction of how Gallegina had backshot Benjamin Threekiller.

"How long will this last, Skye?" asked Anna. Her arm pressed warmly into his as they sat in the row immediately behind the prosecutor at his table.

"Do you want to get back to Seth?" he asked. Fargo worried that Anna avoided his direct questions about her brother's condition. Whether fever or some other ailment incapacitated the young man. Fargo had expected to see him in the courthouse alongside his sister. After all, their father's killer was on trial.

"He . . . he will be all right for a while," she said vaguely. Fargo had seen how distant and withdrawn she had become. When he had first met her, Anna had been vibrant and alive. Now she seemed distracted by the most trivial things—and her mind was always somewhere else. He began to wonder how serious Seth's illness was. Seth had been weak and confused after Watie released him, but Fargo saw nothing more wrong with him than simple exhaustion.

Before Fargo could say anything more, Chief Ross rapped for silence and ordered the trial to begin. The preliminary evidence was scanty, but Fargo quickly found himself on the stand, sworn in and facing the assembled citizens of the Cherokee Nation. The burden of proof lay on his broad shoulders. He knew Gallegina had cut down Benjamin Threekiller and had to speak convincingly enough to sway the jury.

Fargo heard the prosecutor ask a question but he missed it.

"Mr. Fargo, are you deaf?" asked John Ross.

"Chief Ross, in the back of the room. There!" Fargo cried, pointing. "One of McGhee's gang!"

The outlaw shoved a woman aside and kicked open the double doors leading from the courtroom. This produced more than a ripple of comment. John Drew stood and barked orders. A half-dozen troopers from the Light Horse Brigade rushed after the outlaw, creating even more chaos in their departure.

"Order, I'll have order!" barked John Ross. But his

words were drowned out by an explosion at the side of the room. Fargo was thrown across the judge's desk, and Ross toppled from his chair onto the floor. The chief moaned and was slow to get up. Fargo scrambled to his feet, looking up in time to see Thomas and two of McGhee's men shove the defense attorney out of the way. They shot off Gallegina's chains and pushed him toward the gaping hole in the side of the courtroom where they had dynamited the wall.

Fargo's hand flashed for the Colt at his hip, only to find an empty holster. Expecting trouble, Ross had ordered all firearms to be surrendered before anyone entered the court. Now it worked against him and everyone else. The outlaw, with Fargo's unwitting help, had lured Drew's militia from the room. By now they might be halfway to the Kansas border chasing a decoy while Thomas and the others freed Gallegina.

Fargo ducked as Thomas spotted him. The gunman let loose with a couple shots.

"Stay down," Fargo told Chief Ross as he moved around the judge's desk. He reached down and plucked out his Arkansas toothpick. The old chief started to say something about weapons in the court, but Fargo gave him no choice. He reared up, tossed the knife and then dived to land under the prosecutor's table.

"You son of a bitch," came Thomas's grating curse. "I want you, Fargo. I want you dead, you bastard!"

The table turned to splinters as the outlaw shot repeatedly at Fargo. Fargo tried to remember how many rounds Thomas had fired but couldn't. All he really knew was that cowering behind the table was the surest route to the graveyard. He had to attack if he wanted to stay alive.

But how? He had thrown his knife and had not stopped Thomas. He took hold of the table legs and heaved, then pushed hard. Fargo used the table as a shield as the drove hard across the couple yards separating the prosecution from the defense. The table quivered as Fargo smashed it into Thomas, knocking him to the floor.

Fargo tried to get around the table and almost lost the top of his head when Thomas fired pointblank. Fargo feinted to see if he could draw more fire from Thomas.

The deputy's six-shooter came up empty this time. Fargo wasted no time jumping over the overturned table. He landed hard on Thomas's chest, but the man's anger kept him from being injured. Fargo reached out and gripped the handle of his knife stuck in Thomas's shoulder. As he pulled it out, he twisted hard to inflict the most pain he could.

He wanted Thomas to give up. He wanted Thomas to surrender and stand trial. But the outlaw deputy was too ornery for that. He kicked at Fargo and knocked the Arkansas toothpick from his grip. Fargo made the mistake of watching his knife skitter across the floor. This gave Thomas the chance to rear up and swing his six-gun. The heavy barrel caught Fargo alongside the head, stunning him.

Pain rang in his skull like the sound emanating from a bell. Fargo had thought his head wound had healed. He was wrong. All along the spot where Delacroix or Thomas had shot him earlier now glowed white-hot. His vision blurred, but Fargo was as cussed as Thomas—and even more determined.

He leaped after his knife, knowing Thomas's six-shooter was empty.

"Here, Thomas, take this!" came the shout from outside. Fargo looked up to see a rifle sailing through the air. One of Thomas's cohorts had tossed him the rifle. Fargo felt his heart hammering fiercely in his breast. Every movement seemed dipped in thick molasses and the summer day turned unnaturally icy.

Thomas swung the rifle around as Fargo reached for his Arkansas toothpick. Flinging the knife underhanded at the same instant a white puff of gunsmoke billowed from the rifle bore, Fargo was released from the spell that held him. He twisted fast and still felt hot lead cut into his side. He slammed hard to the floor and looked up, waiting for Thomas's second shot.

The outlaw stood with the rifle clutched in his hands,

but he stared down stupidly at the middle of his chest. Fargo's first throw had only wounded Thomas. This time he had hit him squarely in the chest. The blade had slipped between ribs and cut through the man's foul heart.

Thomas gurgled and slumped to the ground like a marionette with its strings cut.

Only then did Fargo hear the uproar in the courtroom. Everyone seemed to be shouting at the same instant, but it was Anna who came to his side.

"You're wounded, Skye. I'll get the doctor."

He looked at the wound and knew it was not serious. He bled like a stuck pig, but it would scab over fast because it was shallow. He sucked in a few tentative deep breaths, then stood. No pain. He had lost a few inches of skin and some blood but nothing more.

Not like Deputy Thomas, who had lost his life.

"Stay back," Fargo said, pushing Anna around so she wouldn't be in the line of fire. He grabbed the rifle from Thomas's lifeless fingers and cautiously went to the ragged hole the gang had blown in the side of the courthouse. Peering out left him feeling as desolate as he had ever been.

McGhee's gang had again successfully rescued Gallegina. He saw Drew and his men milling in confusion around the streets by the courthouse when they should have been riding hard and fast after the fleeing road agents. They hadn't caught the decoy in the courtroom or any of the men who had taken part in rescuing Gallegina.

They were worse than useless. They were in the way of everyone else who might have prevented Gallegina's rescue.

But this time Fargo was determined that Benjamin Threekiller's killer would not evade justice a third time.

14

Fargo stared down at Thomas's body. He had been sent into Indian Territory to capture the McGhee gang and hadn't realized at the time both deputies riding with him were in cahoots with the outlaw leader. Delacroix was toiling as a slave in Stand Watie's fields and now Thomas lay dead at his feet.

He heaved a deep sigh when he realized how little he had really accomplished since riding into the Cherokee Nation. Twice he had nabbed Gallegina for Threekiller's murder and twice McGhee had sprung the man. Fargo realized he might have been going about it all wrong. Cutting off McGhee and recapturing Gallegina would have been easier.

"You've got to get him, Skye. Please," sobbed Anna, clinging to him. He did not understand why she was so upset. The fuss in the courtroom had happened fast and the only one to be injured was Thomas, unless Chief Ross's bruises were considered an injury. Fargo had already forgotten about the nick on his side. The doctor had grunted, swabbed the wound with carbolic acid and then bandaged him.

"I will," he promised.

"You've got to hurry to do it. Gallegina can't be allowed to ride around free for long. He . . . he just can't," she finished lamely. Fargo wondered what she had started to say.

"Go back to the farm," he said gently. "Tend to Seth." This caused the lovely woman to tense in his arms.

"Very well," she said, her voice again a thousand miles distant. Anna turned from him as if she wanted to say something but did not know how. Fargo wished he could make it easier for her because he worried that whatever she had to say was important.

Anna left the courtroom without so much as a backward look at him.

"We done good, men," bragged Pathkiller, strutting around with his thumbs stuck in his vest and puffing out his chest. "We stopped them cold."

Fargo had seen how celebrity affected some men. Pathkiller was riding high on public adulation, and it wouldn't do any good to point out that Gallegina had escaped, that none of McGhee's gang had been captured, and that Thomas was dead only because Fargo had carried his Arkansas toothpick into the courtroom.

John Drew came up and waited for Pathkiller to give him a salute. This was about the full extent of military discipline in the Light Horse Brigade. Fargo stepped back and then left the men to clean up the mess. It would take several days to repair the hole blown in the side of the courthouse. By then Fargo intended to have Gallegina back to pick up his trial where they had left off.

"And Mustang Jack McGhee. He had to catch the elusive outlaw captain, too. Not only had McGhee murdered Coot, he had brought about a whirlwind of death and destruction since coming to Indian Territory.

"Mr. Fargo, may I have a word with you?" Chief Ross stood in the doorway of his office, leaning heavily on a cane.

"Chief," Fargo acknowledged. "I'm in a powerful hurry to go after Gallegina. If this can wait— "

"It cannot," Ross said, the timber of his voice such that it rumbled throughout the foyer. He hobbled into his office and collapsed on the sofa. He watched as Fargo entered and closed the door behind him.

"So?" asked Fargo, anxious to get on the trail.

"Go back to Arkansas. Judge Ringo can use you in Fort Smith. Here among the Five Civilized Tribes you are nothing but an embarrassment."

"An embarrassment to you? To Stand Watie? To the Light Horse Brigade?"

"Don't be impertinent. You know what I am saying."

"You want to forget this. You want to sweep Three-killer's murder under the rug so you don't have to deal with it."

"It is vexing, that I freely admit. He was a loyal follower, but bigger issues occupy my time. You do not understand the undercurrents of Cherokee politics."

"I don't understand Cherokee justice if you're willing to let Gallegina go unpunished."

"He will meet his end one day and pay for his deeds in the hereafter," John Ross said, seeming to age before Fargo's eyes. "I simply cannot continue wasting my limited resources on him."

"You don't have to. I'll bring him back. I know I can't take him to Fort Smith to stand trial since a crime committed in Indian Territory isn't considered to be one across the Mississippi, but I swear Gallegina will be brought to justice."

"I don't cotton to killers, Fargo," Ross said, an edge returning to his voice. "If you kill him, I will see that you stand trial for his death."

"I want him alive so I can see him drop through the trapdoor on a gallows," Fargo said. He saw no reason to bandy words with Chief Ross. "I'll catch him—*again*—and you can try him— *again*."

Before Ross could say anything more, Fargo jerked open the door and left. He stood on the front steps of the courthouse and let the hot summer sun beat against his face until sweat beaded. It felt good to be alive when Thomas had come so close to killing him. It would feel even better when he brought Gallegina back to finish his trial.

The gang had hightailed it out of Tahlequah heading west toward Fort Gibson, but they quickly turned north to avoid any possible encounter with the cavalry. Fargo followed their trail until he came to a crossroads. The best he could tell, three or four riders continued north while a single horseman turned eastward, as if doubling back. He had misjudged how diabolical McGhee was on previous occasions, and Fargo vowed not to do it again, but the single rider bothered him.

He dropped to the ground and studied the hoofprints more carefully. Every detail of the horseshoes leaving the prints was filed away in his memory. For some reason he could not put into words, he felt this was Gallegina's track.

As he rode, sometimes having to pick out distinctive marks left by the horseshoes amid the welter of others left by earlier travelers, Fargo decided he was on the right course. Gallegina returned to land he knew rather than riding with McGhee's men.

The familiar hills around Tahleqah fell behind, replaced by those near the Threekiller farm. The farmlands had been cleared for acres and acres in a pleasant green valley now partially hidden by gathering mist. Fargo felt the change in the air and looked at the dark clouds building in the sky. Rain was on its way soon.

He picked up his pace, not wanting the rain to wash away the tracks he had followed most of the day. Fargo looked around and knew Gallegina must have a hidey-hole in the area where he felt safe. As Fargo studied the hills and the valley between, the first drops of rain spattered on his face.

Fargo wiped them off and knew he had to find Gallegina some way other than tracking. Gallegina lived in the hills, possibly where he could see the Threekiller farm and let his resentment against Benjamin grow. That explained how he found it so easy to gun down an old man minding his own business. Whatever bad blood there was between Benjamin and Gallegina had not sprung up overnight—and Benjamin might never have known Gallegina's true feelings.

The rain came harder now, forcing Fargo to pull down the brim of his hat to protect his face and keep his vision clear. He thought about going to the farmhouse and waiting out the storm with Anna, but Fargo knew that wouldn't do. She had not been herself at the trial. Perhaps it was only grief for her slain father, but Fargo thought her distress went deeper. She had come to grips with the loss of her father but not with Seth being so sick.

The rain beat faster on the brim of his hat, forcing Fargo to seek shelter under the overreaching limbs of a tall oak. The rain fell in blinding sheets now, blocking off the terrain all around him. Fargo tethered his Ovaro and sat to wait out the tempest. At least no wind whipped the rain around corners and under his clothes. The constant drone of rain on the leafy canopy over his head allowed him to think.

The best conclusion he could reach was that Gallegina lived up on a ridge where he could see the Threekiller farm. Maybe the man had a letch for Anna. That made sense—as it made sense she would have nothing to do with a slacker like Gallegina. Or perhaps Gallegina had one of the innumerable blood feuds with Benjamin.

Or Seth.

Fargo couldn't discount that since both men were about the same age they might have locked horns.

"To the ridge above the farm," Fargo said to his Ovaro as the rain lessened. He waited another fifteen minutes for the heavy rain to let up to a drizzle and then led the horse from the dubious shelter under the tree. By the time he rode for the ridge, it had become nothing more than a mist turning the land even greener with its life-giving moisture.

He headed straight up the muddy slopes and got to the ridge. Fargo rode around a short while until he found a spot overlooking the Threekiller farm. A slow smile came to his lips when he saw a well-used path leading to a wooded area a few dozen yards away. Before he reached the stand of trees he heard a horse whinnying. Fargo dismounted, drew his Colt and approached the trees cautiously.

A lean-to had been constructed using a tree as support. Gallegina crouched under the canvas flap and warmed his hands on a fitful fire. Everything Fargo had thought was true. Gallegina lived here, spying on the Threekillers, possibly lusting after Anna but not having the courage to court her outright.

"If you've got a gun and go for it, I'll cut you down where you sit," Fargo said. Gallegina looked up, startled. His eyes darted from side to side as he looked for a way to run again.

"Don't shoot me!" he cried, falling back on whining and pleading. Fargo restrained himself from pulling the trigger when he heard the man's tone. Gallegina was nothing but a skulker and lacked a spine.

"This time you won't get away because McGhee will be in the next cell."

"You caught him?"

"The whole gang," Fargo said, trying to weasel as much information out of Gallegina as he could. "The Light Horse Brigade caught the lot of them in their camp out by Watie's farm."

"Watie's Farm? But it was north of Tahlequah." Gallegina's eyes widened when he realized he had let the cat out of the bag.

"Thanks," Fargo said. "Now let's get back to court. This time no one will blow up the courthouse to save you."

As Gallegina stood, he gripped the edge of the canvas and jerked hard. As he did, he somersaulted around behind the tree. Fargo fired and sent splinters flying, but he missed the fleeing Cherokee by a country mile.

"Don't do this," Fargo called. "I'll catch you again. I've done it before." His words fell on deaf ears because Gallegina knew what he would return to in Tahlequah. Fargo wasn't sure if dying by a bullet out in the countryside wasn't a better end than swinging at the end of a hemp rope.

That's what made him all the more determined to take Gallegina in. The Cherokee deserved the harshest punishment the law could mete out. Humiliation because he had been sentenced to hang was part of the penalty for murdering Ben.

"You were spying on Anna Threekiller, weren't you?" Fargo called, trying to flush his quarry. He turned wary as he went after Gallegina. He had not seen the man pick up a gun, but he didn't want to be wrong—dead wrong.

121

"She spurned me. Her father drove me off like a dog," Gallegina cried, furious. "They said I was no good. But I watched. She was not so good either."

Fargo homed in on the sound from a bush a few yards deeper into the woods. He circled, alert for any movement. He saw a dark figure crouching behind brambles as he came up from the side. Gallegina heard him, turned and fired. Fargo hit the ground, belly down, and returned fire.

"Give up, Gallegina."

"I am no longer a Cherokee. I deny my heritage."

"Fine, have it your way. Give up, Buck," Fargo said, switching tactics. It did no good. Gallegina fired frantically, the slugs whining through the forest. Not a one came close to Fargo, but he remained on his belly. He was counting. Four shots.

"You will never take me alive!" Gallegina stood, presenting a perfect target for Fargo. Fargo saw the man wanted to die right here. And Fargo was not going to oblige him. Putting his Colt on the ground, Fargo dug in his toes and rocketed forward, coming in low and hitting Gallegina in the belly with his shoulder.

The Cherokee gasped and fell, his six-shooter sailing out of his hand. Fargo cocked his fist back, ready to punch out Gallegina, but it wasn't necessary. Gallegina cried openly in defeat.

"You kill me. Don't let them hang me."

"You murdered Benjamin Threekiller. You're going to pay for that." Fargo grabbed a handful of shirt and pulled Gallegina to his feet. Seldom had he seen a man as beaten. He shoved him along, bent and retrieved his six-shooter, though he doubted he would need it now.

"Where's your horse?" Fargo asked. Gallegina pointed vaguely.

"Let's go get it. I want to get back to Tahlequah as fast as I can."

The horse was tethered to a limb of a tree some distance from Gallegina's lean-to. He shook his head and turned sullen.

"I will do nothing. You cannot make me."

"Reckon not," Fargo said. "I can shoot you in the leg. Then I can shoot you in the other leg and drag you back all the way." He had no intention of doing it but wanted to get Gallegina to cooperate. Fargo did not care if the Cherokee liked it—he never would—but he was tiring of the man's petulant ways. There was nothing about Gallegina or the way he lived his life that Fargo liked.

Fargo pointed his six-gun at Gallegina's leg and made like he as going to shoot. But it was Fargo who jumped when the shot rang out.

Gallegina's mouth opened and then closed like a fish flopping out of water along a stream. Then he fell forward, dead before he hit the ground.

Fargo stared at his six-shooter, wondering what had happened. His Colt had not discharged, but as blood poured from the Cherokee's chest, he knew that Gallegina was clearly dead.

15

Fargo stared at the six-shooter in his hand, then shook himself free of the strange spell. He had not fired. That meant someone else had gunned down Gallegina. Fargo looked up, past the corpse and into the woods. He saw nothing. He heard nothing. Gallegina might have been killed by a ghost flitting through the green canopy of leaves and leaving behind only destruction.

At the thought, Fargo looked up into the limbs of the trees. He thought he saw unusual movement and began walking slowly in the direction of the shaking clump of leaves. He pointed his six-shooter up and then relaxed when a pair of thrush exploded out of hiding. All he had found was a birds' nest. Looking around and straining every sense availed him nothing. Gallegina's killer had struck and then faded into the forest without a trace.

Fargo returned to the dead man. Getting his feet under him, Fargo heaved and got Gallegina's bulky body up and over the back of his horse. It took almost five minutes for Fargo to secure the corpse with a diamond hitch so it would not fall off. Only then did Fargo retrieve his Ovaro.

Swinging into the saddle, Fargo set off to find Gallegina's killer. He fastened the reins of Gallegina's horse behind him on the cantle so he could hunt more easily for any trace of the backshooter who had ended Gallegina's life the same way Gallegina had ended Benjamin Threekiller's. Whoever had drilled Gallegina from behind was a good woodsman and had covered his tracks well.

More by instinct than firm evidence, Fargo rode along

the top of the ridge and slowly went down into the valley holding the Threekiller farm. He looked up when he saw the small whitewashed house, the red barn and the stock tank beyond it. Memories flooded him, good ones—and bad.

He had not enjoyed telling Anna and Seth their father had died any more than he would enjoy telling them their father's killer had been gunned down. Riding slowly, he made his way toward the house and did not stop until he was in front of the porch.

Before, Anna had always come rushing out to greet him. Not now. Fargo dismounted and led the horses around to the side. He saw no reason to burden Anna with the sight of the corpse. She had been through so much already.

He went back to the front of the simple white house, wondering if the lovely woman and her brother were even home. By now the squawking chickens and the braying mules in the barn should have alerted them that they had visitors. He lightly jumped to the porch, but before he could knock, Anna opened the door. Fargo tried to understand the expression on her face and found himself at a total loss. She was flushed as if she had run a mile but her breathing was normal. The dark-haired beauty looked at him with frightened eyes, but when she spoke there was no tremor in her voice.

"Skye, I thought you were out on the trail hunting Gallegina."

"I found him," he said.

"Then you've come to—" She stopped in midsentence, as if changing her mind about what to say. "Then you've come to take me back to town for the trial." The words sounded lame. He wondered what she had intended to say.

"Gallegina is dead. Shot down."

"You killed him?" The question carried the same lack of conviction.

"Someone else did. I had the drop on Gallegina and a bushwhacker shot him in the back."

"McGhee," she said forcefully. "The man is a monster. How Gallegina could throw in with him is beyond me."

"Might have been McGhee," Fargo allowed. "John Drew's militia still hasn't caught up with the gang yet." He looked past her into the house. The front room was in disarray as if someone had searched it hurriedly. She saw his attention was fixed on the mess.

"Oh, Skye, my house is so unkempt. I haven't done any housekeeping since Seth . . . since Seth fell ill," she said. "Let's not go in. It's so much nicer outside, anyway. The heat, you know."

"It is hot," he agreed, allowing her to lock her arm in his and lead him down the steps.

Anna sighed heavily as she stared at the cool, inviting stock tank. "We had fun there, didn't we?" she said, as if she were ran old woman remembering a wild childhood fling. "We could again."

"This isn't the time, Anna."

"Oh, I didn't mean in the water again. There, Skye, let's go sit under the shade of that tree. The rain cooled things off a mite, and it is so wonderful outside."

She steered him toward a huge oak tree with limbs stretching out ten feet. Anna half turned and looked up into his eyes. Then her eyelids closed, and she pursed her lips.

"Kiss me, Skye. I need you so. Especially now."

He did not ask why she wanted him now because she did not wait for him to respond. She reached up and locked her fingers through his thick hair to pull his face to hers. The kiss was savage. Ever ounce of desire locked within her comely body poured forth to ensnare him. Fargo tried to resist and then surrendered to her need.

Arms around her, he drew her closer until she crushed passionately against him. He felt the woman's hard nipples poking through her thin bodice. She was aroused and getting more so with every second they kissed. His lips parted slightly, and Anna's tongue rushed forth to tangle with his. Those tongues dueled erotically until Fargo found himself responding to her desperate overtures.

"You taste so good, Skye," she said. "Let me see if you do everywhere." She grinned wickedly, then began opening his shirt all the way down his chest. When she got to his gun belt, she nimbly stripped him of it and began working on the buttons of his trousers. His manhood sprang out, hard and throbbingly ready for her. Anna bent forward and took the knobby end into her mouth.

Fargo went weak in the knees as her mouth moved all over him. Up one side and down the other. She lavished kisses everywhere. Her tongue stimulated him until he ached with need.

"No more," he said. "I want—"

"You want what I want," she said, pushing him flat on the ground and hiking her skirts as she straddled his waist. He felt her hands working under the billows of cloth as they sought his hardness. Anna gripped him and guided him to her fragile nether lips. The woman was ready for him. She rose slightly, wiggled her hips and then lowered herself slowly. His shaft sank fully into her clinging, moist interior. When she had taken him fully, Anna closed her eyes and threw back her head like a frisky filly. Her long dark hair floated like a banner on the wind as she began twisting slowly from side to side.

Fargo gasped with the intensity of the hot sensations working their way from her most intimate recess, through his fleshy stalk and down into his loins. Reaching up, he cupped her firm breasts in both hands. He quickly pushed away her dress to reveal the twin globes of coppery flesh capped with dark nips. Using thumbs and forefingers, he caught both buds and began tweaking them. Anna sighed in pleasure.

He knew right away how exciting she found this. Her heart hammered faster, and the female sheath surrounding him tightened until it felt like a hand in a soft glove crushing down. Fargo caught both breasts fully in the palms of his hands and pressed until the rubbery nipples rested on his palms. Then he began rotating the twin mounds of flesh. This drove Anna wild with desire. She began rising and falling on his fleshy piston, turning to and fro as she went. Fargo forced himself to lie still on the ground, no matter how much he wanted to thrust. He enjoyed this and did not want to ruin the lovemaking.

"So good, Skye. So big inside me," Anna sobbed out. She tossed her head again and reached down to press her hands against his, causing her breasts to flatten even more. Then she reached behind her and under her skirts, fishing for the hairy bag under his thick stalk. Massaging there sent lightning bolts of desire blasting into Fargo.

"I can't do right by you this way," he said.

"Y-you're doing fine," Anna insisted. "Make it last. Keep going as long as you can. Please, Skye, please!" The pleading carried an oddly plaintive note to it. She did not speak out of lust but something else. Fargo couldn't make head nor tail of it and didn't want to try.

He kneaded her breasts and then worked slowly down the woman's sides with his fingertips until he came up behind, cupping her rump. He kneaded the firm round half-moons like they were lumps of dough. Pushing and pulling them apart, he caused her hips to explode in a frenzy of movement.

"Yes, oh, yes, no, yes!" she cried out. Anna leaned forward, her hands pressing hard into his shoulder as her hips began moving with more speed and determination.

Fargo loved the feelings building within him, but he needed more. Being pinned below her was not enough. Hands gripping her behind firmly, he sat up. She let out a squeal of surprise as he continued his forward movement, bearing her to the ground so Anna lay flat on her back.

Her legs parted wide and lifted to either side of his powerful body. Fargo positioned himself on his knees as he looked down into the woman's eyes. Anna quickly shut her eyes, either out of unbridled passion or—what?

He began a slow, steady movement that plunged him far into her wantonly yielding interior. Once fully hidden away within Anna, he ground his hips into hers. Anna gasped and moaned and responded with what seemed like real unbridled passion for the first time. She hunched up to try to keep him within her molten core as he deliberately backed out. When the thick knob on the head of his organ parted her nether lips, Fargo plunged back in. Anna let out a scream of delight.

Faster and faster he pistoned, building heat along with desire in them both. Anna's body shuddered constantly now, and when she arched her back and let out a long, low cry of release, Fargo knew he could not keep going much longer. She squeezed down on his buried length like a collapsing mine shaft.

He grunted and began moving with hard, fast, short strokes that rapidly pushed him past the limits of endurance. He grunted and arched his back trying to split her apart as he spilled his fiery seed. Fargo was not sure, but he thought Anna responded with equal fervor a second time, and then she sagged to the ground, sweating and flushed.

Fargo rocked back onto his heels and looked down at the attractive woman. The flush on her face now was subtly different from that when he had seen her back at the house. How, he could not say—but it was different.

Just as making love to her had been unlike earlier times together. She had an almost frantic need for him this time that he could not explain. Whatever drove her, it was not lust or even simple longing to be close. She had a different motive.

As that thought crossed his mind, the pieces of the puzzle fell into place.

"Where is he?" Fargo asked.

"What?" Anna's dark eyes went wide with fright. "I . . . I don't know who you mean."

"Seth. He's not back at the house, is he?"

"He's out somewhere. He was feeling better and—"

"Don't lie to me," Fargo said sharply. "You weren't all that shocked when I told you someone had plugged Gallegina. You knew your brother had shot him, didn't you?"

"Don't be absurd. You don't know what you're talking about."

Fargo watched as Anna angrily pulled shut the bodice of her dress, hiding the breasts he had enjoyed so much. She pushed down her skirts with a finality that Fargo had to accept.

"He murdered Gallegina when I had him in custody," Fargo said. "That makes Seth a murderer, just like the man he shot."

"The man who backshot our father!" she raged.

"Gallegina would have hanged for it," Fargo said. "You saw how the judge and jury were leaning. There would never have been any mercy in that court, not with John Ross presiding."

"Where's the justice?" she raged, kicking at him and scuttling backward like a crab. Anna drew her legs under her, crossed her arms and spun away, staring off across the fields behind the barn.

She looked in that direction; Fargo looked back toward the farmhouse. Everything Anna had done since he rode up with Gallegina loaded like a sack of flour on his horse had been intended to distract him. Fargo had to admit she had done a good job.

"Is Seth in the house?" he asked.

"Skye, don't. No!" she cried, turning toward him to clasp his arm tightly. "You don't know about him. He hasn't been right in the head since Watie held him captive. I don't know what those monsters did to him, but it hurt Seth. And I don't mean his body. It's his mind that's hurting!"

"You mean he's gone crazy?"

"No, yes, oh, Skye, I don't know what's happened to him. He's not responsible for what he does."

"He has to stand trial. Chief Ross is a fair man. I don't know what Cherokee law is like on this, but I'm certain he'll protect Seth's rights."

"Skye!" Anna grabbed for him, but he pulled free. He buttoned his trousers and slung his gun belt around his waist.

"Skye, don't do it. Don't. I swear, I'll hate you forever if you take him in."

Fargo saw no alternative to doing the lawful thing. It wasn't his right to pass judgment over what Anna's brother had done to Gallegina. He took a deep breath and went to the farmhouse, hunting for Seth Threekiller.

16

Fargo touched the butt of his Colt and wondered if he needed to draw it. From the way Anna acted, her brother was hiding somewhere nearby. If he had gone crazy as she claimed, Seth was doubly dangerous and unpredictable. Fargo and the young man had never hit it off too well, in spite of how he had rescued Seth from Stand Watie's clutches and had dóne all he could to bring Gallegina to justice.

"Seth, run!" shouted Anna. "Fargo's coming after you. Run!"

Fargo knew better than to look behind him. Anna meant to distract him so her brother could get away—or bushwhack him as he had already done to Gallegina.

Movement inside the house gave Seth Threekiller away. Fargo left his six-shooter in its holster as he mounted the steps to the front porch and peered into the once neatly kept house. It looked to Fargo as if Seth was the one responsible for tearing up everything, and he now stood in the doorway leading to the bedroom holding a ripped-apart pillow that showered goose feathers everywhere.

"I have to take you into Tahlequah," Fargo called. "Don't make it worse by fighting. Your sister's explained everything, and I'll do what I can to see that you don't hang."

"He was bad, and he wanted to do bad things to Anna," came Seth's anguished cry. He ducked back into the bedroom and dropped the pillow. Fargo watched the slow fall of feathers and was almost caught flatfooted. The young man came from the bedroom, a rifle clutched in his hands. His hair was mussed and the wild look in his eyes told Fargo how deadly Seth had become.

"I know what's happened, Seth. I'll tell Chief Ross. He'll understand. You won't hang. You might go to prison for a while, but you won't hang." Fargo was not sure of that, but he meant it when he said he would do whatever he could to help Seth.

Seth let out a cry more like a rabid animal than a human as he lifted the rifle and began firing. Fargo threw himself to one side of the porch, letting the farmhouse wall take the slugs intended for his body. The lead ripped huge chunks from the wall, and then there was only silence.

Fargo chanced a quick peek around the doorjamb. Seth had vanished. Taking a deep breath, then letting it go in a rush, Fargo spun around and dashed into the front room. Seth was nowhere to be seen. Resting his hand on the butt of his Colt, Fargo went exploring. It took less than a minute for him to see that the house was empty.

It was as if Seth had turned to mist and had floated away invisibly on the wind.

As he walked across the floor of the front room, Fargo figured out what had happened. He examined the flooring and quickly found a trapdoor leading to a root cellar. The darkness below promised only death if he ventured into it. Fargo looked around but didn't see any way he could light the cellar.

"Seth, I'm coming down," he said. Fargo dropped, not bothering to use the splintery ladder. He hit the dirt floor in a crouch, expecting to dodge more than bullets. All he heard was the gasping breath of a man a few feet away.

The pale square of light above illuminated the cellar just enough for Fargo to see Seth Threekiller huddled in the corner, sobbing. The rifle he had used to kill Gallegina—and almost kill Fargo—lay on the dirt floor. Fargo kicked it away, then grabbed Seth's arms and lifted the man. He did not resist.

"Let's take a ride into Tahlequah," Fargo said. Seth did not argue.

*   *   *

A hundred times as they rode into the Cherokee capital Fargo thought of just letting Seth go. Anna's vile words and curses as they had left the farm burned in his brain, but he could not let Seth go even to appease her. The man's mind had snapped, and there was no telling what danger he posed to himself and those around him. All he had done as they rode was mutter and look around as if someone were chasing him.

Fargo looked from the fearful Seth to the dead body bouncing on the back of the horse behind him. Seth had to answer for Gallegina's death, even if he had gone crazy and thought he as justified in killing his father's murderer.

Fargo knew what was right and did it, but that didn't make him any happier. The crowd along Tahlequah's main street stood silently and stared as he rode directly to the courthouse and dismounted.

"We're here," he said gently to Seth. He reached up and tugged at the man's sweat-soaked sleeve to get him moving. Seth had become increasingly animal-like during the ride but now stood straighter and seemed to understand what was happening.

He preceded Fargo up the steps and went into Chief Ross's office without saying a word.

Fargo could not help glancing toward the side of the courtroom where McGhee's gang had blown the hole during their rescue attempt of Gallegina. The carpenter had done a good job fixing the ragged hole, but Fargo still saw where the dynamite had ripped out the wall. He heaved a sigh. There would be rescue this time, not for Seth Threekiller.

Other things were different for this trial, also. Anna Threekiller sat on the far side of the courtroom, as far from him as she could get. She had her arms wrapped tightly around herself, in spite of the stifling heat inside the room. He had tried to talk to her before Chief Ross had rapped the trial to order, but she had pointedly ignored him. She refused to forgive him for bringing her brother in, no matter that Seth was a danger to himself—and to her. All the young man had to do was have his fevered brain convince him his sister was also a danger or had turned on him or was really their father's killer. Nothing had to make sense to turn against her because he was no longer responsible for his actions.

Seth sat alongside the same attorney who had defended Gallegina. The prosecutor rolled a pencil from one side of the table to another, obviously wishing he were anywhere else. None of the Cherokees were keen on bringing charges against Seth.

Fargo hoped this meant the young man would get the help he needed.

"We have serious charges before this court today," Chief Ross said. "From the statements on record, there is only one witness to the crime."

"Alleged crime," piped up Seth's attorney.

"Point taken," John Ross said briskly. The old man looked more in control today than he had previously. "Mr. Fargo, please take the stand, and let's get this over with." Chief Ross mopped at his wrinkled face with a white linen handkerchief.

Fargo was sworn in and the prosecutor asked a series of questions Fargo could not answer about feuds between the Ross and Ridge parties, represented by Stand Watie.

"So you claim to know nothing of the bad blood between Mr. Threekiller and Gallegina?"

"Seth knew Gallegina had killed his father," Fargo said.

"Was Gallegina not a member of the Watie faction?"

Fargo shrugged. He neither knew nor cared. He doubted Watie wanted anything to do with the likes of Gallegina, but he had no direct knowledge. This was not relevant to the matter of pulling a trigger and shooting another man in the back.

"Gallegina killed Benjamin Threekiller, then Seth avenged his father's death," the prosecutor said. "That sums it up, doesn't it, Mr. Fargo."

"Seth has been out of his mind with grief," Fargo said. "And he was in Stand Watie's custody for a few more days. After he got home, he was never quite right in the head.''

The prosecutor said nothing to this.

"No more questions," Chief Ross said from the bench.

"Isn't the defense attorney going to ask anything?" Fargo said, surprised at the way the trial was going. It almost seemed as if the lawyers' roles had been reversed in some peculiar fashion.

"Since it is widely known that Gallegina's sympathies were with Watie and his criminals, it is not surprising someone supporting the rule of law in the Cherokee Nation would be aggrieved," John Ross said. "Further, carrying the unfortunate death of his father so long in his breast surely affected a dedicated son like Seth Three-killer. Taking all this into account, I hereby levy a fee of $100 against Mr. Threekiller for court costs." Chief Ross rapped his gavel smartly.

"Wait," Fargo said. "He *killed* Gallegina. He shot him in the back."

"What is your reason to protest my decision, Mr. Fargo? I found him guilty. Isn't that what you wanted?"

"He's not right in the head. And if you think he is, you should have sent him to prison for a few years. He shot a man in the *back*."

"Justice has been served. Gallegina was never properly sentenced. I would have considered hanging the murderous son of a bitch," John Ross said, his cheeks flushing with anger. "I consider it only carrying out the nation's will that Seth killed him."

"He shot him in the back," Fargo repeated. He looked into the throng and saw Anna and Seth leaving.

"I don't understand your problem, Mr. Fargo. Didn't you testify that he needed help?"

"Yes, but—"

"Miss Threekiller is skilled and can minister well to him," John Ross said. He glared at Fargo, indicating this was the last he wanted to hear on the matter.

Fargo experienced a momentary whirl of confusion. Everyone—including himself—argued at cross-purposes. Seth deserved to be sent to jail but not hanged. But such a small fine and nothing more when he was a danger to everyone around him? To Fargo it seemed Ross was more interested in putting Stand Watie in a bad light than he was in punishing a crime.

And he might have been. Politics made for bad law.

Fargo left the stifling courthouse and stepped into the hot summer sun. He squinted and looked around. The crowd was already dissipating, running for shade and a cool drink of water or lemonade. He knew he should partake of some of that water, but doubted anyone in Tahlequah was going to be overly polite to him now.

He took a deep breath, then let it out. He had come to Indian Territory to track down Coot Marlowe's killer, and this was a chore that still needed doing. Being sidetracked with Benjamin Threekiller's murder and the politics around it had only slowed him, not stopped him. He went into the street, wondering how he was going to nab the elusive Mustang Jack McGhee. Fargo had already found the deputies sent by Judge Ringo were either members of the McGhee gang or had been bought after they crossed the Mississippi, and they had been punished.

Of the two, Fargo thought Thomas was better off. He was dead while Delacroix toiled in Stand Watie's fields.

"Are you leaving now?" asked Pathkiller.

Fargo looked around. He had been so deep in thought that he had not heard the Cherokee approach him.

"I'm going after McGhee," he said. "He's slipped out of our hands too often. It's time to bring him to justice."

"You will not find him in Indian Territory. Leave our nation. Go back to Fort Smith and tell your judge never to send lawmen here again."

"Is that a threat?" Fargo did not react well to intimidation. If anything, it added more steel to his spine and hardened his resolve.

"You do not belong here. Go home."

"Where do you reckon McGhee ran off to after we failed to capture him and his cutthroats? The time I caught Gallegina?" Fargo knew he poured salt into Pathkiller's wound and did not care.

"Hell," Pathkiller said coldly. "You will find him in

of the unfairness. Gallegina was no prize, but he deserved his day in court and Seth had robbed him of that.

Worst of all was the way Chief Ross had let Seth off on the murder charge simply because a Ross supporter had killed one of Stand Watie's supposed men.

Fargo wondered if Watie even knew who Gallegina had been. For all the beef he had with Watie, the man had a strict code of justice that Fargo doubted extended to letting killers off, no matter their political alignment. Seth should have been sent to jail, not given a piddling fine and released. More than this, Seth needed someone who could get him back on track and chase away the demons of craziness.

"Sitting here's not finding the gang," Fargo said to his Ovaro. The pinto bobbed its head and snorted in agreement. It had eaten its fill of the juicy buffalo grass growing on the hillside and was ready to travel some more. Fargo mounted and made his way down the slope into the valley, choosing to ride in the direction opposite to that taken by the Light Horse troopers.

He came onto a road and looked up and down it, as if he could see the ends. Fargo paused when he saw flashes of red plaid moving. Coming to a decision, he turned his horse in that direction and walked along the muddy road until he came upon two men struggling to get their wagon unmired from a particularly deep mudhole.

"Can I give you a hand?" Fargo offered.

"I don't know if it'll amount to a hill of beans," grumbled one. "They done took everything that's worth anything."

"Who's that?" Fargo asked, riding around and studying the situation.

"Outlaws. White men," said the other Cherokee, eyeing Fargo suspiciously.

This perked Fargo up. He described Mustang Jack McGhee and saw from the men's expressions who had robbed them.

"What were you carrying?" he asked the teamsters.

"A considerable bit of foodstuffs. Flour, beans, a couple barrels of sugar and lard. They took it all."

"McGhee'll eat like a prince tonight," Fargo said. He stopped behind the wagon, tossed the end of his lariat down and said, "Fasten that around your axle. With my horse pulling and you two putting your shoulder to the wheels, we can get it out in jig time."

The Ovaro strained and dug in its heels as Fargo urged it to begin pulling. With a sudden surge, the wagon came free and Fargo fought to keep the horse from hurting itself pulling the wagon along the road.

"Thanks, mister," one Cherokee said, sitting in the empty bed and swinging his short legs. "Now we don't know what to do next, 'less you want to help out."

"What can I do?"

"They took our team," the other teamster said. "They took everything but our shirts, truth to tell. Can you let 'em know over at Stand Watie's farm what's happened?"

"You Watie's men?"

"That we are, and he's not going to be happy losing this much food."

"Him?" laughed the other teamster. "His son'll skin us alive. That Saladin's a pistol."

"I'll let them know," Fargo promised. "When did the outlaws rob you?"

One man squinted as he peered into the sky. Then he shoved a stick upright in the mud and studied the shadow it cast. Only after his friend had gone through the same procedure did the first man speak.

"Two hours back, just past one o'clock. Five of them. By now they got our beans all cooked up and are making bread."

"How'd they make off with barrels of sugar?" Fargo asked.

"They had a wagon of their own. Since ours was bogged down, they made us move our cargo to their wagon. I hope Watie cuts their tongues out. They was a rude bunch, even for a lot of road agents."

"I'll get help out to you," Fargo promised, riding around until he found the twin ruts left by a heavily laden wagon heading out across Cowskin Prairie. He itched to follow, but he had promised the men he would have Watie send help for them.

He got directions to Watie's farm from the men, then galloped that way, anxious to fulfill his promise and get on McGhee's trail. Barely had he gone two miles when he saw signal mirrors at work from low hills on either side of the road. Someone had spotted him and signaled ahead that he was on his way. Fargo was not surprised when he came across a small band of armed men waiting for him in the center of the road around a sharp bend.

"Mr. Fargo, we've been expecting you," said Saladin Watie. The young teenager seemed in easy control of the much older armed men riding with him.

"I saw your scouts' mirrors. You've got quite an intelligence network."

Saladin only smiled and waited for him to explain his presence.

"McGhee's gang robbed one of your supply wagons. The drivers are unhurt but madder than wet hens about two miles back down the road."

"The food," grumbled Saladin. "My mother had promised to make an apple pie when she got the flour, too." He motioned and three of the armed militiamen with him headed in the direction Fargo had come. "They will do what they can."

"Will you help me track McGhee?" Fargo knew he faced five outlaws. Going it alone was dangerous, but if Watie's men joined him, he stood a good chance of capturing them all. "When I catch McGhee, I'll get him back to Fort Smith and you'll have one less thorn in your side."

"I'll have one more apple pie to eat," Saladin said. "But I cannot spare anyone at the moment, Mr. Fargo. John Drew's bandits are moving north from Tahlequah, and I dare not let up my vigilance for one second."

"What are they doing? I saw a dozen of them a few hours ago heading away from here."

"My father's not sure. He's sent my Uncle Elias to talk with John Ross, but that's a fool's errand. If shooting starts, you do not want to be caught between our guns. John Drew's men might not be such good shots, but I assure you my father's are excellent marksmen."

"Then I'd better catch McGhee and get the hell out of Indian Territory," Fargo said.

"That you should, Mr. Fargo. I wish I could help, but my duty lies in a different direction. Perhaps one day I will be free to go after such trespassers."

With that Saladin Watie rode off, his men at his heels. Fargo shook his head in amazement. For such a young man, Saladin was quite a leader. If the Cherokees could ever stop their squabbling, he wold grow up to be a chief and maybe even a principal chief of the nation.

Fargo cut across the prairie, intending to cross the wagon tracks quicker this way. It took almost fifteen minutes of hard riding before he found the deep ruts marking the passage of McGhee's wagon. Circling the tracks. Fargo tried to estimate how many men rode with the wagon. The teamsters had said five outlaws had robbed them, but Fargo made out more tracks in the soft ground.

Mustang Jack McGhee had come to Indian Territory not only to hide out but to recruit for his gang. The more of them that died and were caught, the bigger the gang got by recruiting others on the run.

Fargo rode along cautiously, knowing McGhee was aware of the deep ruts left by the wagon and how easily followed it would be. He had to know of the animosity between the factions in the Cherokee Nation—and he had to know how effective Stand Watie's vigilantes were. McGhee might not care whose supplies he stole, but he would not want to tangle with Watie.

McGhee had eluded Pathkiller and the Light Horse troopers more than once, but Watie? Getting a determined Watie on the trail would end the outlaw's career.

Fargo rode slower as the sun set on the far edge of Cowskin Prairie. He finally dismounted and waited until dusk gathered, cloaking him in shadow, before proceeding. He needed all the luck in the world if he wanted to catch Mustang Jack.

The acrid odor of burning cow chips made Fargo's

nose wrinkle, warning him he neared McGhee's camp. Rather than continue following the wagon ruts, Fargo left his horse and advanced on foot to scout the outlaws' campground. He walked past one guard before he even realized there was anyone near.

Fargo went into a crouch, his hand resting on the handle of his Colt. His response wasn't needed. The guard had his back against a rock and snored softly. McGhee would have the man's ears if he knew he had fallen asleep on guard duty. Too many times the alert sentries had saved the outlaw leader's hide.

On cat's paws, Fargo made his way down until he was within twenty feet of the camp. Fargo flashed on the last time he had been this close to McGhee. The scene was almost identical. Mustang Jack used a twig to draw a map in the dirt, stabbing with it and pointing and drawing long, sweeping curves as Ned Sondergard and another of McGhee's lieutenants looked on.

The smell of cooking food made Fargo's belly rumble a mite. It had been a while since he had eaten a decent meal. He knew the fixings for this one had been stolen from Watie's larder, but that wouldn't much matter. The aroma was mouth-watering and distracting.

He forced himself back to studying how to snatch McGhee out from under the noses of his men. Again, fighting the entire camp was out of the question. Even if Saladin Watie had brought his small band of armed men, the fight would have been a hard one. Fargo counted no fewer than ten men in the camp.

No wonder McGhee needed supplies. He was building an outlaw army.

"Cut off the head and the body dies," Fargo said softly as he circled the camp, coming up to the south of the spot where McGhee had spread his bedroll.

Fargo edged forward when McGhee flopped on his bedroll, hands under his head, and stared at the stars poking out into the ink-black curtain of night. Fargo froze when McGhee suddenly sat up and called, "Lucas! Lucas! Get your ass over here!"

A man who looked more like a mountain lumbered over and stood at the foot of his boss' blankets.

"Whatya want, Jack?"

"I've got an itchy feeling that something's not right. Are the sentries out?"

"All of 'em. I caught that worthless cow flop Lassiter sleepin', but I woke him up good."

"No one's seen anything unusual?"

The big man shook his shaggy head. "Nuthin', Jack. I swear."

"What about Watie's men? The ones you spotted on the road? Are they after us for stealing their food?"

"Naw. Tompkins and Bennett came runnin' back and said they never left the road. They got their empty wagon 'n dragged it along. Busted an axle, from the sound of it. But that's only a little kid tellin' 'em what to do."

"That little kid's smarter than the lot of you combined," Mustang Jack said sourly.

Fargo remained frozen, not daring to move a muscle. He wanted to lie flat, but to do so would draw attention. Better to look like a lumpy rock in the darkness than to change position with McGhee being so edgy. And for all his brutish appearance, Lucas sounded as if he was no man's fool.

The slightest miscalculation, the smallest underestimate of his enemies' abilities, would buy Fargo an unmarked grave out here on the prairie.

"You worry too much, Jack. You got the orneriest, hardest ridin', straightest shootin' owlhoots ever to rob a bank all around you. Nuthin's gonna happen."

"I get jittery when I'm planning a new robbery, especially one this big."

"Hell, Jack, the only thing you got to worry about is how big a wagon are we gonna need to haul off the money!"

"Kansas City will never be the same when we breeze in rich and ready to spend all our loot," McGhee said. "Get on out of here and let me get some sleep."

Fargo waited for Lucas to return to the campfire and take a tin cup of coffee from Sondergard. Lucas and

Sondergard obviously discussed Mustang Jack's fears by the way they occasionally glanced over their shoulders in his direction. Not daring to move as long as they kept looking his way, Fargo settled down to wait.

He was a good hunter and could remain motionless by a game trail all day long, if need be. He pushed those skills to the limit now, since he was relatively exposed. If Lucas or any of the others saw him so much as twitch a muscle while he was in plain view, they would come investigate. But they did not.

After a few minutes of joshing, they turned back to tending their fires, cooking more victuals. When Lucas tore into another plate of beans, Fargo made his move. He eased forward until he came to the top of McGhee's bedroll. This was the closest he had never come to the man who had cut down Coot Marlowe.

A quick move, fingers pinching nostrils shut and a hand over his mouth—that would be all Fargo had to do to snuff out Mustang Jack McGhee's miserable life. Let his gang find him dead in the morning, wondering what had happened.

That was the easy way, but it wasn't the right way.

Fargo moved silently until he came to McGhee's side. The outlaw leader's slow, even breathing told him he was asleep. Fargo cast a quick look over his shoulder to be sure Lucas and the other outlaws were occupied with their tall tales and bountiful food, then moved to take McGhee prisoner.

"Who might you be?" asked McGhee, his six-shooter centered between Fargo's lake-blue eyes.

18

Fargo wanted to cry out, to bolt, to back away from the six-shooter only inches from his face. To have made any move would have meant his instant death.

As cool as a Rocky Mountain breeze, Fargo said, "I came to join up. I heard you have the best gang west of the Mississippi."

"What?" The frown on McGhee's face and the shift of his thoughts from plugging Fargo to dealing with someone who wanted to join his gang of outlaws tripped him up.

Fargo grabbed fast, caught McGhee's wrist and forced the six-gun away. He pinned the outlaw's arm to the ground with his knee and used both hands on McGhee's throat to throttle the man.

"Make even a tiny sound and I'll break your neck," Fargo whispered.

"Hey, Jack, you want somethin' to eat?" bellowed Lucas. "We got plenty!" This produced a round of laughter as the road agents recounted how they had come by their bounty. "Jack? Jack?"

Fargo chanced a quick glance over his shoulder and saw trouble coming. The mountain of gristle and mean rose from his spot beside the cooking fire and started in Fargo's direction. The darkness would protect him only so long. Lucas would see what was going on and raise the alarm.

Even if he didn't, Fargo wasn't sure he could handle both McGhee and his grizzly bear of a lieutenant at the same time.

"Jack?"

McGhee reached over with his free hand and grabbed at Fargo's shirt, yanking hard. He didn't unseat Fargo but succeeded in getting his gun hand free. Fargo squeezed down hard to cut off any outcry, but it didn't make a difference. Lucas saw what was going on.

"The boss is in trouble!" Lucas shouted.

Fargo let up on his grip around McGhee's throat. The outlaw leader gagged and turned onto his side to puke. This gave Fargo all the opening he was likely to get. He grabbed McGhee's fallen six-shooter, rolled and came to his feet shooting. The first two rounds from the road agent's six-gun hit Lucas square in the chest.

To Fargo's surprise, Lucas recoiled as each slug hit, but the man kept coming. If anything, the two bullets angered him rather than slowing or killing him. Fargo fired three more times. The last bullet whined off Lucas's chest, as if the man were made of rock. The final time Fargo shot, the hammer landed on an empty cylinder. McGhee carried his six-shooter with only five rounds for the sake of safety.

"Jack, you all right?" bellowed Lucas.

The huge man lumbered forward like a bad dream. When others in the gang began shouting questions, Lucas turned slightly to wave them to his aid. It was then that Fargo saw the reason why his bullets had no effect on the massive man.

Fargo drew his own Colt, cocked it and aimed squarely between Lucas's eyes.

"Take one more step and I'll blow the top of your head off. You don't have an iron plate there."

"I got one in my head, too," growled Lucas. His shirt hung open, revealing a thick metal plate tied to his chest. Not even a rifle bullet would have penetrated that armor, but a single shot to the head would bring him down fast.

"I don't care if you've got rocks in your head," Fargo said, reaching down and grabbing McGhee's collar. He pulled the still-retching man to his knees. "One shot is all it'll take to stop you." He was aware of the confusion in the outlaw ranks. Whatever he did had to be done fast or he was a goner.

Fargo yanked hard on McGhee's shirt, getting the man to his feet. He was weak but able to walk.

"We're riding out," Fargo told McGhee. "You make any move to escape and I'll drill you."

"Kill me and they'll rip you apart. Hell, you'll wish that's all they did to you. Lucas there's part Apache. He knows ways to torture a man you have never even heard about."

"Maybe I ought to just shoot him now and remove that threat," Fargo said. He saw that McGhee cared nothing about Lucas or any of the others in his gang. He was thinking only of how he could get free.

"You said you wanted to join up. I can pay you more than any bounty hunter would collect for my scalp. Five hundred dollars. You can buy a passel of drinks and whores with that kind of money."

As McGhee dickered, trying to find Fargo's price, Fargo half-dragged him toward the rope corral where the outlaws had tied their horses. Fargo felt as if his attention was being pulled in a dozen different directions. He had to keep watch on McGhee, but Lucas posed a more immediate threat. He had to shoot accurately to hit the man in the leg or head. Any body shot would only produce yet another ricochet off the metal plate strapped to his chest.

Then the others in the gang were getting their wits about them. Ned Sondergard was taking charge, getting them focused on the task of rescuing their leader. Fargo wished he could take them all in, but right now simply staying alive counted for more. He could deal with them after he got away—with Mustang Jack McGhee as his prisoner.

"Saddle your horse," Fargo ordered McGhee. The outlaw was regaining his strength and starting to get a feisty look in his eye. Fargo buffaloed him with his six-shooter, driving him to his knees. Stunned, McGhee looked up at him. "Hurry up."

Fargo fired point-blank when Lucas decided he had to act now or lose his boss for good. The first round pinged off the outlaw's boiler-plated chest. The second caught him in the leg, causing him to fall like a giant redwood being sawed down.

"You son of a bitch. You shot me!" cried Lucas.

Fargo ignored him. Bringing down Lucas had stopped the rest of the outlaws. They huddled together, trying to figure out what to do now. From the look of it, Sondergard saw a way to take over the gang. If McGhee was captured—or dead—that paved the way for a new leader. If their confusion faded and they acted together, Fargo was lost.

Fargo saw McGhee had his horse saddled. He motioned him up into the saddle. McGhee had barely mounted when Fargo whipped out his Arkansas toothpick and severed the rope line tethering the rest of the horses. It took a second slash before he was sure all the horses were freed. He vaulted into the saddle behind McGhee, put the knife to the outlaw's throat and then fired his six-shooter twice more.

The unfettered horses reared and pawed at the air before bolting into the night.

"Back that way," Fargo ordered, using the knife across McGhee's throat to indicate the direction he wanted the man to ride. The chaos left behind him wouldn't last long. Sondergard or Lucas would take control eventually, get the men chasing after their horses and then the fun would begin.

Fargo wanted to put as much distance between him and them as he could before that happened.

"I—" McGhee yelped as Fargo jumped from behind him to land astride his Ovaro. As he vaulted to his own horse, Fargo left a thin red cut on McGhee's throat.

"That's a little of what you can expect if you try to escape," Fargo promised. He sheathed his knife and then pointed his six-shooter at the outlaw. "Ride back to the road where you robbed the wagon."

"I don't know which way that is," McGhee said, stalling. Fargo fired next to the man's head. The hot gunpowder burned McGhee's ear, and the report deafened him. He got the idea that Fargo wasn't joking. He turned his pony's face in the direction of the road and took off at a trot, Fargo on his heels.

Fargo knew better than to gallop across the prairie at night. It was easy enough for a horse to step in a prairie dog hole in daylight, but at night the odds were doubled. He kept McGhee in view as he leaned back, fumbled in his saddlebags and finally found the oilskin pouch holding a fully loaded cylinder for his Colt. He knocked out the cylinder in his gun and replaced it with a fully loaded one.

"I offered five hundred," McGhee said. "I'll make that a thousand. No reward on my head is that high. You'll be rich, and who's to know you got bought off?"

"I'd know," Fargo said, settling his Colt back into his holster. "No amount of money's enough to rob me of the pleasure of seeing you swinging from a gallows."

"You make it sound personal. I don't know you from Adam."

"You killed my partner."

"Hell, partners are a dime a dozen. I'll make it fifteen hundred. I got the money, and it can be yours. Take all I got. Must be damned near two thousand dollars."

"My partner's memory is worth more than you've got or ever will have," Fargo said. He clamped his mouth shut. Talking about Coot Marlowe riled him, and he needed a clear head to get away. He knew McGhee would never give him a plugged nickel and only played for time. Sooner or later his gang would get their wits about them and come hunting for the man who had kidnapped their boss.

When they did, Fargo intended to give them a little surprise.

They reached the road where Watie's supply wagon had been robbed. To the south lay Tahlequah and to the north Stand Watie's farm in the middle of Cowskin Prairie. Fargo turned toward the north, doubting he could find any support with John Ross. The principal chief had made it clear enough that Cherokee law was for Cherokees, no others need apply. Stand Watie was more the privateer in his thinking, cruising out on the prairie with his militia trying to keep the peace as he saw it. If they shot an occasional supporter of John Ross, all the better, but Fargo had the gut feeling Watie was a better ally at the moment.

Even if he was a slaveholder.

"You can't ride all night," McGhee pointed out. "My horse is getting tired. I damned near rode it into the ground earlier, and it's cruel to make it carry me much farther."

"I can shoot you here and let the horse rest all it wants," Fargo said. He canted his head to one side, listening hard for the sound of pursuit. The still night carried many sounds, but from what he heard he knew McGhee's gang was on his trail. Fargo picked up the pace, forcing McGhee to push his horse.

"You think you can find sanctuary at Stand Watie's place?" asked McGhee, when he saw the direction they rode. "Think again. He nabbed a deputy from Fort Smith and has him working like a slave in his fields."

"You ought to know since Delacroix is one of your gang," Fargo said. For a moment, McGhee was silent. Then he laughed.

"Not much gets by you, does it? Yeah, Delacroix was one of my boys. He got careless."

"So did Thomas. He stepped in front of a flying toothpick while you were trying to rescue Gallegina."

"What a fool. I told Thomas we should have let the son of a bitch swing, but he said I needed somebody to act as go-between for us while we were hiding out. Gallegina spoke Cherokee, at least, but that was about all the talent he had except screwing up everything he tried."

Fargo's mind raced as he planned. McGhee's gang had reached the rod not a half mile back and would soon figure out the direction they had taken. One thing McGhee had said that was true— his horse was wobbling as it walked. Trying to outrun the gang was out of the question.

Fargo pointed and got McGhee off the road and down

into a ravine. The sun was already poking pale fingers of pinks and grays above the horizon. He had to work fast.

"Look, I'm going to spring a big raid. That bank in Tahlequah is itching to be robbed. The entire Cherokee Nation's treasury is there. Damned near fifty thousand dollars, if Gallegina was to be believed."

Fargo finally heard the real reason McGhee had been so willing to rescue the backshooting Cherokee. He had knowledge of how to rob the largest single bank in all Indian Territory.

"We can take it, you and me. We don't need the rest of them yahoos. They're dumb. They—"

McGhee grunted as Fargo swung his rifle. The barrel caught McGhee alongside the head, knocking him from his horse. He lay flat on his back on the ground, unconscious. Fargo wished he had time to make sure the outlaw wasn't going to come to and hightail it before he got back, but there wasn't time for that.

He put his heels into the Ovaro's flanks and galloped back to the road and then turned toward Stand Watie's farm. Fargo reached the rise in the road before it curled down to the farm. Not a half mile away camped Watie's militiamen. He lifted the Henry rifle to his shoulder and calculated the arc it needed for a bullet to reach the camp.

Then he fired. Again and again he fired until the magazine was empty. For a short time it sounded as if a war had started. A few of the slugs spanged into trees near the camp. Otherwise, no one in Watie's vigilante posse was much in danger. Fargo waited to make certain they were out of the bedrolls and saddling their horses, though, before he raced back down the road, then cut off and found the ravine where McGhee struggled back to consciousness.

"Wha—?"

Fargo slugged him again, then draped him over his horse's back like a sack of flour. He led the horse down the ravine running at an angle from the road until he reached a stretch where he could ride directly east toward the Mississippi.

As McGhee again came to, groaning and sagging from being bounced on his belly. Fargo heard gunfire that made his few shots sound like wet firecrackers. Stand Watie's men had plowed straight into McGhee's gang. If he had to bet, Fargo would place his money on Watie's militia.

The closer they got to Fort Smith, the more sullen Mustang Jack McGhee became. Fargo was content to ride along in silence, wrapped in his own thoughts. From the first time he had ridden into Fort Smith to meet Coot, nothing had gone the way he had thought. The idea of going into Indian Territory with Coot to play the bounty hunter had not appealed to him as much as being on the trail again with his old partner.

That had all evaporated in a flash of gunfire. Fargo glanced at McGhee. He had wrapped the man securely but had let him ride with his hands bound in front of him so he could hold onto the saddle horn. Fargo didn't much care if McGhee had been unable to stay on his horse and had been thrown off, but taking the time to get him back into the saddle would have lengthened the trip.

Fargo wanted an end to this. With McGhee at the end of the hangman's rope.

They rode into Fort Smith with no hint of interest from the residents they passed. Unlike Tahlequah, this was not a town where every citizen knew the others. Too many people came and went for such intimate friendship. That suited Fargo fine right now. He didn't want to stop, talk and explain what had happened to everyone along the road leading to the large brick building where Judge Ringo held court.

"You're making a big mistake, Fargo," McGhee said as he was pulled from his horse. "You're passing up a lot of money. There's still time. I have it salted away back in Indian Territory."

"There's nothing for you there anymore," Fargo told him. He was pretty sure Watie's militia had wiped out the outlaws, but even if they hadn't, the McGhee gang was scattered and not likely to cause any more trouble.

"Ned, Lucas and the others don't know where I hid the money. We've been raiding for months and months. And the Tahlequah bank. Think about getting a cut of that much money, Fargo. You'd be a rich man. I have it all planned. We hit the bank, then hightail it to Kansas City and spend it until we're drunk and broke."

"I'm already a rich man," Fargo said, although he didn't have two nickels to rub together. "I'm rich in knowing you're back where you belong." He shoved McGhee up the steps.

Now people began to notice. A whisper started and spread like wildfire, going all the way into the courthouse. By the time Fargo got McGhee to the top of the steps, four federal marshals and Judge Ringo were waiting.

"Brought you a present, Judge," Fargo said, turning McGhee over to a pair of the marshals. Fargo watched the lawmen drag off the outlaw leader. "I also have some bad news for you about Thomas and Delacroix."

"You noticed those were new marshals taking custody of McGhee, didn't you, Mr. Fargo? I think I know what your bad news is about my deputies."

"Both of them were in cahoots with McGhee. I don't know if he paid them off or if they actually rode with him, but they were rotten."

"So were others. No more," the judge said with some satisfaction. "Packer's been reprimanded and told to pay more attention to who he's hiring."

"Thomas is dead, shot down trying to rescue another of McGhee's men while he was standing trial in Tahlequah."

"That does not surprise me," Judge Ringo said. "I will set the trial date for McGhee right away. It might take a week or two to cross all the *t*'s and dot the *i*'s but he will swing. There is a preponderance of evidence against him, especially in the death of your partner since you are an eyewitness."

"Thanks, Judge. If Coot Marlowe were here, he'd thank you, too."

"Are you going to stay in Fort Smith? I can use a man of your integrity."

"I've got an errand to run first, Judge, but I'll be back in time for McGhee's trial."

Fargo took his leave, tired and dusty from the trail, but knowing he had a lot of miles still ahead of him before he could rest.

19

Every muscle in Fargo's body ached, and he was getting tired of the landscape. He longed for the cool, tall mountains much farther west, but had to endure hot, dusty Cowskin Prairie a while longer. He had ridden hard and fast from Arkansas, wanting to finish his errand and return to Fort Smith before Jack McGhee went to trial for murdering Coot Marlowe, not to mention his other crimes.

Thinking on that, Fargo decided he had seen the inside of enough courtrooms to satisfy him for the rest of his life. He had testified and watched Seth Threekiller walk out a free man after shooting Gallegina in the back. Gallegina had deserved punishment, but it had not been the young man's place to mete it out. Fargo had to blame John Ross and Cherokee politics for the failure to deliver justice.

Fargo hoped Anna was dealing well with Seth, but he was not going to ride past Tahlequah or their farm to find out. Those bridges had been burned, and he had no desire to find how they were doing because there was nothing he could do that would benefit either Anna or her brother.

He reined back and turned his head slightly to catch the faint drumming of horses' hooves. Fargo wiped his dried lips and considered what to do. He had avoided contact with the few Cherokees he had spotted on his way back into Indian Territory, not wanting to stir up old hatreds and cause new ones.

He turned his Ovaro in the direction of a deep gully that crisscrossed the prairie, got down into it and continued on his way. The thunder of hooves drew closer, and Fargo finally stopped to wait out the riders. Peering over the edge of the deep ravine, he saw the scouts. A few minutes later came a dozen riders, one of them carrying a military pennant fluttering from a long staff. Fargo frowned as he tried to figure out whose militia this was. He did not recognize the riders, and they were certainly not U.S. Army cavalry from Fort Gibson. None of them wore a complete uniform, although a few sported blue shirts or broad-brimmed hats.

The scouts returned and joined the main body. They milled about, looking over the prairie as if searching for something. Fargo caught his breath. The scouts might have picked up his tracks; they might be looking for him, although no one knew he had returned.

That meant the patrol hunted anyone along the road. They did not care who they sought. It was more important for them to check every traveler if they wanted to regulate opposing factions—whoever might head that faction.

"Watie? Ross?" Fargo could not identify the riders or their loyalty. That they were a ragtag militia was apparent, as was the determination to find whoever had left the road and cut across the prairie—their prairie.

Fargo waited them out. The scouts and the leader argued for several minutes, then the two scouts angrily wheeled about and continued down the road. The leader went through his multiclad force, talking to them and whipping them into shape again. When they rode off, they assumed a more military column, but barely.

The ravine began to peter out after another mile, forcing Fargo back into plain view of anyone riding along the road. But he neared Stand Watie's farm, unseen so far. He circled the main house and came around to the crops in the fields beyond. A dozen slaves toiled, but Delacroix was easy to pick out. The sun had darkened his already swarthy skin, but Fargo knew the deputy would never match the others' complexions.

He dismounted and settled down, waiting for sundown. Fargo gnawed on some jerky and munched on hardtack, washing it all down with a few swallows of tepid water from his canteen. He had more food in his saddlebags, but he wanted to save it.

By twilight, Fargo was well fed, rested and ready to move. The slaves moved from the fields and went into a nearby barracks. Boldly walking down, Fargo kept a sharp eye out for foremen. Inside the barracks the slaves had been fed and one of their number went up and down, counting heads. Fargo waited for him to do his inventory before poking his head inside.

"Mr. Watie wants the Cajun in the main house," he called, then ducked back out. His heart pounded a little faster as he worried that his charade would be discovered. But in a few minutes Delacroix came shuffling out, leg irons hindering his movement.

Fargo moved fast. He clamped his hand over Delacroix's mouth and whispered, "I'm getting you out of here. Don't make a sound."

"Fargo!" exclaimed Delacroix. Fargo clamped his hand back over the deputy's mouth.

"Where is the key to your shackles?" Fargo whispered. Delacroix pointed to a small house a few yards away. "That the overseer's?" Again Delacroix nodded. Fargo motioned for Delacroix to stay put, then went hunting for the key.

He hurried to the small house, peered in the dirty window and saw a man curled up on a small bed, already asleep. Fargo wondered if the overseer had drunk himself into oblivion. It didn't matter why he slept so heavily. What mattered were the keys fastened to a large wire ring hanging by the door.

Holding his breath, Fargo opened the creaking door. At every instant he was certain the man would awaken and raise the alarm. Whatever caused him to sleep kept him from noticing even loud noises as Fargo slipped in, quickly lifted the key ring and then left.

He ran back to where an impatient Delacroix waited for him.

"I thought you would never get back." Delacroix

smiled crookedly. "I thought I would never see you again—or anyone not black or red."

"Quiet," Fargo said, dropping to his knees. He tried one key after another until he found the one releasing Delacroix's leg irons. Freeing the deputy had a curious effect on Fargo. He wanted to laugh and celebrate—and he wanted to refasten the shackles and send the man back to the fields as punishment.

The moment passed. He was doing the right thing freeing Delacroix.

"Do you have a horse for me?" Delacroix asked.

"Get one," Fargo said. "Meet me on the top of the hill near the fields where you worked today. The entire area is filled with Watie's militiamen, and I know the only way out."

"You are a fine fellow, Fargo." Delacroix slapped him on the shoulder. "I misjudged you." Delacroix hesitated. "Where do you go while I get my horse?"

"Business," Fargo said, "that needs to be taken care of." He saw Delacroix hurry off. The deputy might try to elude him but he would not succeed. He could never get enough of a head start. Fargo hurried back to the barracks and went inside. He tossed the key ring to a slave on the nearest bunk.

"Whass this, massah?" asked the slave.

"If you were free, where would you go?" Fargo asked.

"To Creek country," the man said without hesitation. "My brother is a freeman there."

"Get your leg irons off. And see that the others are released, too. Then it's up to you to get out of here."

"Wait," the slave said, working to get the proper key. "Why are you doing this?"

Fargo looked up and down the ranks of bunks.

"Because I have to," he said. He left quickly, hoping the men in the barracks found their way to creek country or Kansas or anywhere they could be free to do what they chose, not ordered about by some slave master, no matter how charitable he might be. From the looks of their conditions, these slaves were not mistreated by Watie—but they were still slaves.

Fargo's long legs devoured the distance up the hill to where he had left his Ovaro. As he suspected, Delacroix was not waiting, but it took him only a few minutes to catch up with the fleeing deputy.

"Oh, it is you, Fargo. I . . . I thought to get well along the road. I knew you would catch up."

"Watie's vigilantes are patrolling in that direction," Fargo said, indicating where Delacroix had been heading. "We're going back that way, across the Mississippi, to Fort Smith."

"A good idea, eh?" said Delacroix, laughing. "I can return to be deputy for Judge Ringo. We can outdo even Mustang Jack, you and I! I will hear of gold shipments and you can rob them. Together, we will become rich!"

"McGhee's already back in Fort Smith," Fargo said.

"Ah, then we can join with him again," Delacroix said, easily shrugging off his treason to his former boss. "You are a surprise, Fargo. I never thought you would want to be a road agent. How I misjudged you!"

That's right, Fargo smiled, figuring that correcting the man would only make things difficult. For once Fargo would do something the easy way. The surprise on the corrupt deputy's face would be priceless once he realized that not only was he going back to stand trial alongside McGhee, but that he had turned himself in as well.

And surprised he was! Three weeks later Mustang Jack McGhee was sentenced to hang, and Judge Ringo sent his former deputy marshal to the Detroit Federal Prison for twenty years.

Only then was Fargo free to ride on, knowing Coot Marlowe rested a little easier in his grave because justice had been served.

LOOKING FORWARD!
The following is the opening section from the next novel in the exciting *Trailsman* series from Signet:

THE TRAILSMAN #239
COMMANCHE BATTLE CRY

South of the Mexican Border, 1858—The trail to wealth and salvation follows the Rio Grande, but the riverbanks are spilling over with hostility as an epidemic of blood threatens to run the river's water red. The Trailsman soon finds out that staying alive is like swimming upriver . . . if the tide doesn't drag you down, the current will.

Fargo dipped his paddle into the smooth crimson water without taking his eyes from the shoreline. He was sure he saw movement somewhere in a stand of slender oak trees on a ridge to the north. Their bullhide canoe swished through the Rio Grande's quiet waters like a knife through warm butter, despite its wide beam. Josh Brooks sat in the prow, muscular arms paddling easily as if he experienced no fatigue from previous days of travel against strong, steady currents northwest of El Paso. His sable skin bore a sheen of sweat catching late day sunlight that gave the tall Creole fur trapper an aura not unlike the dark oiled barrel of the Whitney rifle lying near his feet.

"I'd nearly swear I saw something up yonder," Fargo said.

"This sun can play tricks on a man's eyes," Josh warned as he studied the same wooded ridge. "I ain't seen nothin' move. Maybe it's the light."

It was true, the way a setting sun sometimes brought changes to even the most familiar shapes. It had been a dry fall and the gauzy sun dropped toward the earth through a haze of dust on the horizon. Colored light splashed on bare ground, painting an occasional tree trunk with ocher hues and turning fall oak and cottonwood leaves into sizzling displays of bright reds and dazzling yellows as though they were ablaze. The beauty of a Western sunset never ceased to enthrall Fargo, particularly in this land of flaming reds and softer pastels. Even the land itself was blood-colored, as they traveled farther north. Where the land turned red, they were warned to be on the lookout for natives. *Red land meant red men along this river,* Buckshot Sims, an old friend of Fargo's, used to say. Sims had traveled this river enough to be taken seriously, but then again, Skye Fargo was no stranger to the Rio Grande either.

Fargo paddled slowly, examining the ridge. Once, he glanced down to the Colt revolver lying atop a bundle of traps, its frame mottled by time and weather. The pistol wasn't accurate for any distance, but at close range a properly charged .36 caliber ball made a hell of a hole. For long distance shooting his Henry rifle could center a raven's eye on the wing.

He watched the trees backgrounded by the soft colors of the sky, glazed by gold from the sun with leaves of crimson, orange, burnt umber and lightly freckled browns. Blue shadows formed below leafy limbs that turned to slate where no sunlight penetrated, a soft gray spot here and there, where fading light created the illusion of movement. He couldn't be sure.

The gentle gurgle of Josh's paddle passing through the sluggish current distracted Fargo from a closer look at a shadow beneath a sinewy branch. Another movement flashed and a splash of blue color emerged as a jay flitted from limb to limb, stirring the stillness with the flutter of its snow-edged wings. An oak leaf twisted on a breath of wind and fell from a branch, dancing and trembling as it swirled toward orange-red earth below.

"I'm seeing things, I reckon," he told Josh in a feathery voice tinged with relief. They weren't looking for a confrontation with Indians. In one of the packs Josh had glass trading beads, cheaply-made iron knives and some colorful ribbon, items Fargo liked to carry just in case he needed to play diplomat. Indians liked bright colors and most had need for iron weapons.

"Maybe," Josh remarked softly, squinting in the sun's hard glare, crow's feet webbing around his heavy-lidded eyes while he let his gaze wander upstream. Josh knew the fur business, but he didn't seem to know much about plains Indian tribes.

The burble of water forking around the canoe's prow had a voice all its own and there were times when Fargo didn't even hear it, having grown accustomed to its gentle music after paddling for so long. For almost two weeks they had moved steadily with the sun at their backs each morning. A grizzled boatman poling a raft of logs in the opposite direction told them five days ago that they'd seen the last of civilization at Bell's Hill, a small settlement on the southern bank where Texas-bound travelers bought supplies for the journey into the new Republic. Fargo and Josh had heard stories of the war there, of a continuing fight with Mexico promising to be long and full of hardship.

Again, he saw something move in the forest but this time it was not a bird . . . he was certain of it. "There," he said, pointing to a cluster of oak atop a knob where a feeder steam entered the river. "Look yonder in those trees, Josh. It sure as hell looked like somebody's hidin' in those oaks."

Sunlight streamed through a profusion of three trunks and branches where Fargo was pointing, making it difficult to separate real objects from shadows. Light played off the smooth glaze that covered the oak and cottonwood leaves, making them sparkle like the flickering lights found in sapphires and diamonds, almost blinding with brilliance when leaves turned on breaths of gentle breeze.

"I don't see a damn thing 'cept trees, Skye."

"Maybe it was nothing."

Josh's paddle dipped into dark water, making ripples across the glassy surface. Cattails along the bank bent slightly when a whisper of air moved among them. Fargo watched the oaks steadily, unwilling to entirely dismiss what he'd seen, even though he had no idea what it was.

"Time we started lookin' for a place to camp," Fargo said, turning his broad face toward the south bank.

"Maybe we oughta look on that side, seein' as you're so sure there's somethin' on this side to worry 'bout, "Josh replied smartly.

"I ain't worried. Bein' careful, is all. "It'll be plumb dark in another hour. I'll fry up some catfish for supper."

"I'm gettin' tired of fish. Truth is, I've been sick of the taste of fish for years. If I never saw another fish in my whole life, it'd suit the hell outa me."

"That's what too many years on the river does to you." Fargo had learned that Josh had made most of his money running goods safely up and down the Mississippi avoiding the pirates that terrorized other flatboat captains. "I can boil up some beans, only it's a shame to waste all this catfish meat."

After a sweep of his paddle, Josh lifted a piece of thick line from the water to inspect a squirming yellow catfish trailing along beside the canoe on cord threaded through the catfish's gills. "I guess you're right Fargo. It'd be a shame if we had to feed him to the turtles, or one of them big ol' coons. Biggest coons I ever saw in my life was livin' along the Mississippi. Weighed maybe forty pounds . . ."

Fargo was only half listening. Something had moved again high on the ridge. He shaded his eyes with a freckled hand. One tree in particular seemed highlighted by the sun's radiance as though it ignited like phosphor, a huge leafy torch standing alone among others in the forest. Behind it, behind the dark outline of its trunk, stood what looked like the silhouette of a man.

"See that biggest tree yonder," he said, pointing again to the ridge. "There's a man standin' behind it. I'd nearly swear an oath it's somebody watchin' us."

Josh returned the fish to the river. He stared at the ridge for a time. "I see it now," he said, speaking so softly that Fargo had trouble hearing him. "I reckon it could be a man."

Fargo knew sign language well, it was the easiest way to declare yourself as friendly. He rested his paddle across his lap and gave the sign for peace. Their canoe slowed against the current. He judged the distance at three hundred yards to the tree, maybe less. He signed again when nothing moved.

"Maybe it's only a tree," Josh suggested. "Hard to tell in this light." He picked up his paddle and continued rowing with slow, deliberate strokes.

"It's an Indian," Fargo said. "He's standin' real still so we can't be sure. I figure he's a lookout. He'll go back and tell the others about us. We could have visitors tonight."

Josh wasn't quite ready to agree yet. Paddling steadily, he kept glancing to the ridge between strokes. "Didn't you say we'd know if they was Osages by their shaved heads? That Apaches have long hair braided in single strand down their backs, and Comanches got two braids, only they'll be farther upriver?"

Fargo recalled almost every detail he knew about traveling this river. Back when Josh contacted him about running the Grande, Fargo's stomach turned. For the man they called Trailsman and a seasoned flatboat pilot with experience battling gangs of river thieves and the most brutal weather imaginable in winter, this trek should have held few real challenges, but Fargo knew better. For whatever reason the Rio Grande always brought Fargo bad luck, and if the money hadn't been as good as it was, he would have told Josh to shove it! "Whatever breed he is, he ain't movin' at all, just standin' there behind that tree like he was a part of it." He resumed paddling in concert with Josh as the canoe came abreast of the ridge, gliding silently toward a setting ball of orange-red sun hovering above the river, flaming over the landscape. Changing the angle from which he watched the tree made no visible change in the silhouette beside it.

"Leastways he ain't shootin' arrows at us," Josh said under his breath, "if it is an Injun."

"I suppose we oughta be grateful for that," Fargo agreed, as they slipped past the ridge unmolested. When he looked up at the tree again, the silhouette was gone. Now he was certain it had been someone watching them. "He's gone, Josh. Unless he went to water the cactuses, I think we're about to have some company.

Josh's head turned quickly to the north as soon as the words left his mouth. He stiffened, halting the motion of his paddle abruptly. "Look yonder, Skye," he said, suddenly sounding grave. "You was right, there's five of 'em. They's ridin' scrawny little ponies . . ."

As the canoe drifted past a deep ravine leading down to the river, Fargo saw what Josh had seen. Five bronze-skinned men on small, multicolored horses watched the canoe from a canebrake at the bottom of the wash. Two carried lances with feathers tied to painted shafts. The others had bows slung over their shoulders or resting across the withers of their ponies.

"Sweet Jesus," Josh whispered, his heart pounding. He sat there, frozen like he was trapped in a block of ice for several seconds, holding his breath until he heard Fargo speak.

"I'm gonna give 'em the sign for peace," Fargo said calmly.

He opened his palm and held it forward, fingers together as with his thumb extended. The Indians seemed to ignore him, sitting passively on the backs of their ponies as he continued to give the sign. Straight rays of sunlight made them appear as red as the river, somewhat copper-colored even, after a closer examination.

"Either they don't know what it means, or they just don't care. He said, as they drifted slowly past the mouth of the ravine in full view of the Indians. He continued to hold his hand in the same manner. Stalks of cane teetered in a current of air around the riders, swaying gently behind five lean, bare-chested men. Fargo lived and hunted among most of the tribes that were scattered across the land. He had fought with them and for them, had killed their sons and loved their daughters. As a people they had earned his respect. The Cherokee, the Navajo, the Flathead, the Sioux, the Kiowa and the Arapaho were as much a part of the land he loved as the coyote and the deer. Fargo respected them as much as he did any other people who followed the trail. While he admired their culture and feared their wrath, he felt he understood why they inspired so many tales of terror. These men were quite clearly part of a far more hostile race than the Cherokee or Seminoles. He had the feeling he was seeing something truly dangerous, like a pack of wolves.

They stared at him and he stared back. It was only a feeling, a vague uneasiness he felt when they looked at him, but he was certain that they viewed him and Josh as prey.

"They ain't Osages," Josh said again, sitting motionless as the canoe continued to glide past the ravine. "They's got a whole headful of hair . . . black as crow feathers."

Current tugged at the canoe, slowing it to a crawl. Fargo lowered his hand and whispered, "Keep paddlin'. They don't act like they'll harm us. If we keep paddlin' maybe they'll see we don't mean them harm." He gripped his paddle in two gnarled fists and forced the blade take a deep bite out of the river.

One Indian on a blue roan pony turned his head and spoke to the others, making some sort of gesture with his hand just as the canoe carried them out of sight. Fargo's mouth felt dry and cottony, as they continued westward toward a glowing sunset, watching the river bank for evidence that they were being followed. Now light and shadow became so intermingled in trees lining the river that he found it impossible to distinguish shapes or movement. With his heart hammering he paddled harder while guiding the canoe farther from the east bank, just in case the air filled with speeding arrows or feathered lances. Josh's powerful strokes helped carry them toward the middle of the broad river quickly.

A blazing sun dipped toward the distant Pacific Ocean half a continent beyond them, dropping below a hilly horizon lined with trees where a watery highway stretched endlessly to touch a fiery sky. Fargo worried about the colors, so many reds, like a veil of blood over the land.

But if things went as Fargo planned, he'd be heading back down the river to El Paso in a couple of weeks to collect his mustang ponies with two hundred dollars in gold for his trouble. All he had to do was find beaver country for Josh Brooks and climb back in this empty canoe, traveling with the current, hardly paddling at all . . .